Dearest Sophie,

My Daughter's Boyfriends
A Short Story Collection

Penny Jackson

You are the most lovely friend of all time!

xoxo

The most beautiful girl in the world!

My Daughter's Boyfriends: A Short Story Collection
By Penny Jackson

Copyright 2023 by Penny Jackson
Cover Copyright 2023 by Untreed Reads Publishing
Cover Design by Ginny Glass

ISBN-13: 979-8-88860-082-5

Also available in ebook format.

Previously published:

"My Daughter's Boyfriends" — Winner of *Lilith Magazine*'s Fiction Contest, April 20, 2021

"Shredding" — *Wild Roof Journal*, May 2022

"The First Brassiere" — Hawaii Pacific Review — The First Brassiere - Best of 'Zine Nomination, July 2021, *Beyond Words Literary Magazine*: Reprint of Best Short Fiction, February 2022

"Prince Hal" — Published by *HerStry* — April 18th. Winner of the Eunice Williams Non-Fiction Prize

"Blue Moon on Riverside" — *The Write Launch*, December 2021

"Walk This Way" — *The Flagler Review*, April 2020

"Green Love" — *Twisted Vine Literary Arts Journal*, May 2022

"Directions" — *Adirondack Review*, December 2021

"The Last Camp Social" — *Burningword Literary Journal*, October 2021

"The Elephant in the Bush" — *Lilith Magazine*, July 2018

"Doctor Wales" — *North by Northeast*, August 2020

"West End Girl" — *The Maine Review*, April 2021

"Echo Beach" — *Scarlet Leaf Review*, October 2021

Published by Untreed Reads, LLC
506 Kansas Street, San Francisco, CA 94107
www.untreedreads.com

Printed in the United States of America.

Without limiting the rights under copyright reserved above, no part of this publication may be reproduced, stored in or introduced into a retrieval system, or transmitted, in any form, or by any means (electronic, mechanical, photocopying, recording, or otherwise), without the prior written permission of both the copyright owner and the above publisher of this book.

The scanning, uploading, and distribution of this book via the Internet or via any other means without the permission of the publisher is illegal and punishable by law. Please purchase only authorized electronic editions, and do not participate in or encourage electronic piracy of copyrighted materials. Your support of the author's rights is appreciated.

Publisher's Note

This is a work of fiction. Names, characters, places, and incidents either are the product of the author's imagination or are used fictitiously, and any resemblance to actual persons, living or dead, business establishments, events, or locales is entirely coincidental.

The publisher does not have any control over and does not assume any responsibility for author or third-party websites or their content.

Also by Penny Jackson and Untreed Reads

Becoming the Butlers

L.A. Child and Other Stories

CONTENTS

MY DAUGHTER'S BOYFRIENDS 1
SHREDDING 11
THE FIRST BRASSIERE 13
PRINCE HAL 17
BLUE MOON ON RIVERSIDE 29
WALK THIS WAY 47
GREEN LOVE 49
DIRECTIONS 57
THE LAST CAMP SOCIAL 65
THE ELEPHANT IN THE BUSH 67
DOCTOR WALES 71
WEST END GIRL 77
ECHO BEACH 85

MY DAUGHTER'S BOYFRIENDS

JACK

Jack is Naomi's first boyfriend. They meet the first day in nursery school and are inseparable. He is a red-headed boy with freckles and mischievous green eyes. Jack also likes to wear Naomi's dresses. A lot. Every time I arrive home from work the babysitter says, "Jacqueline is wearing Naomi's ballet tutu again." Jacqueline is how Jack likes to be referred to during his play dates. His favorite outfit is a pink leotard and a pink tutu Naomi won't wear since she hates ballet class. He also favors Naomi's Cinderella costume that her grandmother bought her from Disneyland. Luckily Jack has not discovered my makeup cabinet. Since Jack just lives down the block, I usually drop him off at his apartment near Morningside Park. I am terrified that his father, a sergeant high up in the police force, could arrive at our apartment and discover him.

I am home from a too-long meeting with a magazine editor and my sitter is pale. "I didn't know what to do," she stammers. Jack's father is standing at the doorway of my daughter's bedroom. I slowly walk toward him and peek into the bedroom. Today Jack has chosen Naomi's best party dress, which is a shocking velvet pink with several beaded necklaces. If he wore a black bob, he would resemble a Twenties flapper. Jack's father towers over me. He is still in his police sergeant's uniform. I hold my breath as Jack's father watches his son and Naomi jump up and down on the bed.

"Hello," I say nervously, but I am surprised. Jack's father is laughing. Laughing so loudly that for a moment I think he is crying.

"Holy Mother of God," Jack's father exclaims. "Just look at him! Jack, you're gorgeous. Absolutely gorgeous!"

And Jack's father is right. His son is gorgeous.

PEDRO

Pedro is from Buenos Aires and has already enchanted the entire second grade. According to Naomi, both she, Elisa Schwartz and Rosie Marks all want to marry him. Pedro is such a sensation that the second-grade teacher, Mrs. Levy, has called in an emergency parents' meeting to discuss the discord that Pedro has brought the classroom. It seems that the girls have been fighting over Pedro in the cafeteria, the gym and on the playground.

One would expect Pedro to be a mini–Antonio Banderas, but he is just a soft-spoken little boy with long lashes and shiny brown hair who is obsessed with turtles and doesn't have the remotest interest in girls. Naomi sobs herself to sleep one night convinced that Pedro will marry Sylvia Cohen, who brings food for Pedro's turtle. But her worries are for naught, as it turns out that Pedro's family is suddenly transferred to London. There isn't even a going-away party, but he does leave his pet turtle behind. The turtle is duly taken care of by every single girl in the class until the school custodian turns the heat off one night and the turtle, named Nueva York for Pedro's brief home, dies from the cold.

HARLAN
Harlan is named after the famous science fiction writer Harlan Ellison; his father tells me this at our synagogue parents' night. Harlan likes to read comic books and does not like to cut his hair, so it's as long as that of the girls in Naomi's Hebrew class. Harlan is madly in love with Naomi and brings her scary comics with violent covers of exploding things, which Naomi tolerates. She doesn't really love Harlan, she tells me, but she will let him visit her and draw fantastic creatures in her notebooks. It helps that Harlan tells Naomi that she is beautiful about twenty times an hour. "Every girl needs to be told she is beautiful twenty times an hour," I tell my husband, who as usual is not listening to me but reading his most recent legal brief. One afternoon Harlan is too preoccupied to notice that he is crossing against a red light and is hit by a delivery bicycle. Thankfully Harlan only suffers a broken leg, but his parents keep him home for his recuperation. Naomi doesn't have time to visit him since she is currently obsessed with horses and spends hours in Central Park watching the riders gallop in the bridle path.

When Harlan finally recovers, he has fallen out of love with Naomi, and in love with Jill Kleiner, the rabbi's daughter. Naomi is miserable for two nights and then decides that Harlan was a nerd and develops a crush on Kevin Bacon while watching *Footloose* at her older cousin Rachel's house.

ROGER
Roger is Naomi's first boyfriend who does not live in New York City. They met during an eighth-grade dance at Naomi's sleep-away camp in the Berkshires. Roger lives in Portland, Maine. "I didn't know there are Jewish boys in Maine," Naomi told me. They have long phone conversations in Naomi's bedroom which has a large PRIVATE sign taped on the door. She is lucky she has no interfering siblings. I suspect that for the first time in his life my husband is jealous of a boy who is beginning to resemble a man. Roger has been left back a year in school and technically should be going to high school. A photograph I discover hidden in Naomi's desk shows a giant who actually needs a shave.

One night, Naomi discovers through her friend Sharon whose cousin who, by some incredible coincidence, attends the same Portland, Maine, school as Roger that he is dating not one but three girls at the same time, including a high school junior. The night that Naomi breaks up with him is also the night she has her first period. From then on, whenever she has menstrual cramps, she refers to them as "Roger's Revenge."

JOSH
Josh is the killer. He is Naomi's ninth-grade crush that lasts through the end of twelfth grade. Josh is devastatingly and dangerously handsome—a private school version of Jim Morrison who plays guitar in a band that does terrible covers of the rock songs that I listened to in the 1970s. No one cares about his lack of guitar skills or that he forgets the lyrics. If I were fourteen, I would be mad about Josh too. He is famous for being thrown out of every Hebrew school, and insisted on wearing a leather jacket during his bar mitzvah. Naomi's love is the unrequited kind, the worst. I know that there are mornings she lingers on the street outside his apartment building. I hear her speaking about this to her friends on

the phone and how she has made close friends with all of Josh's doormen. Has Josh ever acknowledged her? I know from my own experiences with boys like Josh that he is too cool to notice anyone except himself. Eventually Josh's parents will divorce and he will move with his mother to Ashville, North Carolina, which is too far for Naomi to follow. Yet he hovers still about her high school years like the weather—it is always there even though it changes.

Several years later when Naomi is in college, I will find a torn napkin hidden deep in her desk with a scrawled phone number and Josh's signature. Did he give this to Naomi or did Naomi find this and keep it to herself as a wish or a souvenir? All I can hope is that Josh at some moment in time was kind to her.

ARTHUR

In eleventh grade Arthur can almost make Naomi forget Josh. He is the child of two Dead Heads who are now doctors, and Arthur with his ponytail, vintage tie-dyed shirt t-shirts and John Lennon glasses could be of a different decade. Naomi who had recently been a punk rock fan with a fake leather jacket and blue dyed bangs has become a brunette again and favors hemp necklaces and clove cigarettes. She has confided in me about the marijuana plants that grow on the roof of Arthur's parent's townhouse, and claims she doesn't smoke pot because her contacts dry out. Her father, who is now my ex-husband, is not so sure. We had a good divorce if you can have a good divorce. Naomi spent most of her time anyway in Arthur's huge Greenwich Village townhouse, so it was as if she had divorced us too. One night, Naomi arrives home with flushed cheeks and announces she is no longer a virgin.

"But I thought you would have done it already," I stupidly say.

Naomi's mouth pops wide open.

"Do you think I'm a slut Mom?" she shouts.

"But surely don't all you girls…"

She slams the door before I can discuss birth control.

HARRY

Harry is Naomi's college boyfriend for all four years. They meet during freshman orientation and stay together even the last semester of senior year. They are a wonder to their friends and their parents. Harry irritates my ex-husband by his constant grins and guffaws. He is the ultimate frat boy who cannot walk down the street without at least eight people giving him a high five. I do not understand how Naomi, after Arthur, can stand him. But Naomi has turned into a sorority girl with cute pink terrycloth skirts and white tennis sneakers and blonde streaks in her hair.

Even in winter Harry wears flip-flops, t-shirts and shorts. He is from Aspen and has the sharp chiseled features of his mother, a famous Swedish model, with blue eyes and high cheekbones. Harry is almost too pretty at times, and he seems to compensate this by always looking as grungy as possible. "Hasn't he heard of deodorant?" my annoyed ex mumbles to me during Parents Visiting Day When Harry is accepted at business school in California my ex and I share a bottle of champagne. Surely this is the end of a too-long romance.

But we didn't have a real reason to worry. I receive a phone call from Naomi the night before her college graduation.

"Harry's come out," Naomi announces.

"Excuse me?" I ask, not sure about what I heard.

"Harry's gay, Mom. I'm glad for him. I guess I kind of knew."

I don't ask any more questions. At graduation Naomi poses with Harry and they embrace in front of the camera as if they are still a loving couple.

Two years later I will see Harry in a film, and then another film and another. But he has never admitted he is gay, although Naomi knows all about his string of lovers. Every time I see him in *People* magazine with his "new" fiancée, I have to laugh. I never thought Harry was bright, but I never took him for a coward.

OWEN

Owen is married. He is married with two beautiful kids and a beautiful wife. Naomi met Owen at the art gallery where she now works, and he asked her to the Metropolitan Museum for advice since he knew nothing about art. There, in front of a Rembrandt, Naomi fell madly in love with him. Owen is twenty-five years older than Naomi and married to Jessica Carmel, a well-known opera singer who travels all over the world. So, there isn't much to hide from Owen's wife since she is so rarely in New York. But still. Owen is married, and I am the mother wolf.

I follow Owen from work one day (he also works in publishing and I know his office) and confront him directly outside Radio Music City Hall.

"I am Naomi's mother," I tell him. "Please leave her alone."

Owen stares at me for a moment, switches off his mobile phone and sighs. He is a very handsome man with grey, neat hair and very blue eyes.

"I know it's not fair," he answers. "It's wrong, but I don't know what to do. She has threatened to kill herself if I leave her."

I take the train to Brooklyn and immediately ring Naomi's buzzer. When she opens the door, she is eating a yogurt and wearing sweats. She does not look like a suicidal young woman.

"Is it true?" I ask her. "Would you really kill yourself if Owen left you?"

She nods solemnly. I fight the urge to call the police, her father, my husband. The stricken look on her face is the same I saw in eleventh grade when she waited hours to see Josh and his band, and he walked by her without giving her a glance.

But I needn't have worried. Six months later Naomi met Rajiv.

RAJIV

Naomi has quit her job and with an inheritance from my aunt has bought discount around-the-world tickets. She begins in Australia and makes her way through distant continents. In Bombay, she meets a young man from India named Rajiv, an engineer who lives in Jersey City. When she introduces us to Rajiv, they are so in love that they gaze into each other's eyes even when talking to other people. He is tall and funny and loves to cook and sing country western songs. Naomi moves in with Rajiv to his small Jersey City apartment and finds a job teaching art history at a charter school. Naomi's father, my second husband and I are relieved. She has finally found her true love. One afternoon Naomi arrives at my apartment with a bouquet of roses.

"Thank you," I tell her.

"They aren't for you, Mom. They're for Rose. That's why I brought roses."

"Who is Rose?" I ask. Then I see the blush in her face and I understand. She is three months pregnant and instinctively knows that the baby will be a girl. I place the bouquet in my favorite crystal vase and we toast with ginger ale. Finally happiness. She and Rajiv will fly to London to visit his parents. She will be gone for a week and during that time I obsessively shop in every baby store in Manhattan and buy the most beautiful baby dresses ever made.

She is due home the Friday before July 4th. We all plan to watch the fireworks from their Jersey City apartment rooftop. When Rajiv telephones me, I think we have a bad connection because his voice sounds like he's underwater. I hand the phone over to my husband who listens, nods, and then starts to sob.

"My God, what happened?" I scream, but I know. I know. My Naomi is gone. A brain aneurysm on the return flight from London. No one could do anything. These things happen. A famous actor's daughter had suffered the same fate a month ago and the story was in all the papers. I have lost not only my daughter but my granddaughter as well.

Rajiv arrives at our apartment, but I cannot see him. I hear his and my husband's voices outside my bedroom door. I do not leave my bed for three days. Darkness is what I crave. Utter darkness. I lie on my bed, still and silent, like Naomi, like my daughter. Dead yet not dead, which is worse.

THE BOYFRIENDS

Somehow with the aid of drugs and my husband's and my ex-husband's support I make it to the funeral. The rabbi speaks to me but I can't see him in my blur of tears. In one corner of the room I see a group of men. Some converse with each other while others are quiet. There are no women or children with them. All of the men wear beautiful suits. And then I understand. These men are Naomi's past boyfriends. They approach me and one by one embrace me briefly and say a few words. Jack has grown up to look exactly like his father and is an emergency doctor in Maine with twin girls. He's six feet two with a bushy beard and it's so hard to imagine him twirling about in Naomi's shimmery Tinker Belle costume. Pedro, who lives in L.A. and was contacted by a mutual friend about Naomi, is tall and handsome and has long lost his Spanish accent. Arthur, Naomi's long-haired hippie, is now bald and a corporate lawyer in Washington. Harry wears sunglasses to hide his celebrity as well as tears. Owen is here too. He seems to have aged at least twenty years and blows his nose in a monogrammed handkerchief. He tells me he is heartbroken for any pain he caused my daughter. Another man, a good-looking man with dark glistening hair and deep-set eyes approaches me and takes my hand.

"I am so sorry for your loss," he says softly.

"Who are you?" I ask.

"Josh. I knew Naomi in high school."

I stare and stare. The long-lost love of her life.

"You're too late," I say.

"We are all too late," he tells me, rubbing his eyes.

Finally, when the funeral is over, I take the pills the doctor prescribed and tell my husband I need to be alone in our room. But sleep or any sort of relief does not come easily. The only memory that brings me any sort of relief are the faces of Naomi's boyfriends—all of them traveling hundreds of miles to be at her side today. They're not boys anymore—they are men.

I drink a glass of water and walk unsteadily to my computer and begin to write about Naomi. Somehow my girl, my lost girl, has escaped me. Then I wonder if I really did see all the boyfriends or was I just hallucinating? No matter. I am comforted by the vision, real or otherwise, that I witnessed today. I can't bring Naomi back, but I am compelled to write the names of her boyfriends.

Jack
Pedro
Harlan
Roger
Josh
Arthur
Harry
Owen
Rajiv

As I write this list, Naomi appears before me, laughing and shaking her head as she tells me of her latest romantic obsession.

SHREDDING

"Why is that there?" I ask my father, pointing to the bulky black machine on the kitchen table.

He shrugs and turns his back to me. "A shredder. You must have seen them in your office."

My father makes himself busy with the coffee machine, trying to measure the number of grinds for the filter. Since my mother's death eight months ago, he struggles with so many seemingly mundane tasks. Pushing the right button on the dishwasher. Mixing up the bleach with the laundry detergent. A former carpenter, who built our family home, my father's hands have become useless. My sister and I, both lawyers, live in San Francisco. We insisted our father move to California, but he is determined to stay in the New Jersey suburban house he built for my mother in 1957.

"I know what a shredder is," I tell him. "But why do you need one?"

"Because." He spills the grinds on the counter and then hastily wipes it with a paper towel. His hands are now covered with liver spots, the fingers bent slightly with arthritis.

"Because why?"

I don't understand why there is a shredder here. The people who have shredders are often guilty businessmen destroying incriminating documents.

When my father turns to me, I realize his blue eyes are almost colorless. This is what seems to happen to old people with blue eyes. The color, year by year, drains away. My mother's eyes, before she died, were almost as clear as glass.

"Your mother's letters," he tells me as he crumples the dirty paper towel and tosses it into the trashcan. "I bought the machine so I could shred your mother's letters."

For a long moment I cannot speak. Then I ask, trying to control my voice, "Dad, why would you do that?"

"They were private. Isn't that why people buy those machines? For privacy."

"All her letters?"

"All. They weren't meant for you and your sister. They were for my eyes only."

My father moves away from me. He opens the back door and slowly walks down the porch steps to the back yard. I turn to stare at that awful machine. Who would think such an ugly thing, so solid and dull, would be capable of such violence?

My father has murdered my mother's words. All the letters she wrote when he was in Korea. All the letters when her father, a Catholic Irish policeman, forbid her to marry a Protestant. The letters she wrote when she ran away and lived with her sister in Boston, awaiting his return. Two teenagers writing letters of love and tenderness and hope.

It would have been better if my father had collected all her letters and left them in a garbage bag for pickup. Slicing them makes my body feel physical pain, as if my limbs were those letters, violently mutilated. I wonder if I could somehow find all those shredded remains of my mother's words, I could fit them together like a jigsaw puzzle. But I know it's too late. What's gone is gone. Like my mother's mind. She died of dementia. In the end, she did not know any of us. Perhaps this is the reason why my father bought the shredder. To destroy her letters was his way of connecting to her erasure of her past.

I sob for a moment and then wipe my face with a dishtowel. Outside, my father stares at a mound of fresh lawn clippings, which move slightly in the breeze. I open the door and join him in the yard where the late summer grass is still gloriously green.

"I'm sorry," I tell my father.

He nods his head. The breeze has turned into a wind that blows both our hair into our eyes. I reach forward to hold my father's hand that shakes like the leaves in the trees that surround us.

THE FIRST BRASSIERE

The reason why my mother had to buy me a bra was because of a letter from our school's headmaster to the parents of the seventh-grade girls. It was noted that many girls who were "maturing" were not wearing the proper undergarments. Teachers would now routinely check each girl who came to the school by tracing a finger down their backs. If the necessary "item" was not worn, the girl could be sent home.

My headmaster was a bridge partner of my father's. My mother was mortified. I was just confused. They didn't check if boys were wearing underwear. I didn't want a bra. I liked my white undershirts. My breasts were annoying buds that hurt me when I slept on my stomach. The girls who wore bras and had big breasts were teased mercilessly by the boys. I just wanted to be left alone.

That November before Thanksgiving my mother took me to Saks Fifth Avenue. The entire first floor smelled of Charlie, that year's perfume. The doorman had winked at me when we had entered the store, as if he knew of our mission. I hid my face beneath my wool scarf, terrified of running into anyone I knew. The store was hot and already my forehead felt clammy.

The lingerie department was on the top floor, escalator after escalator, as if you were ascending to the top of a castle. I wasn't prepared for so much stuff: pantyhose, girdles, translucent nightgowns, which I knew were called negligees from the romance novels I would read from camp, stockings that looked so fragile that a wisp of wind could knock down the entire rack and then the brassieres. I quickly glanced at them and noticed that many of them had metal hooks and clasps. Instruments of torture.

A saleswoman who wore lipstick the color of dried blood and had hair that looked like a shellacked helmet approached us behind a display of rainbow striped socks.

"We don't want any training brassieres," my mother announced which reminded me of the training wheels on my old bike, which were too big and once ran over my brother's right index finger.

The saleslady squinted her eyes at me—her piercing stare directed at my chest like an arrow.

"Definitely not training," she said. Her voice sounded like she had smoked a hundred cigarettes that morning. She could have been forty or eighty—it was hard to tell because she was wearing so much beige foundation on her face. "Please wait for me in the dressing room on the left," she instructed, waving a hand to a corner of the floor.

"I hate it here," I told my mother who hushed me as we found a dressing room filled with too-bright lights and shiny mirrors. There was one pin on the floor that someone had forgotten to pick up. It looked dangerous. I had a wild fantasy of sticking the saleslady with the pin and watching her mouth open in shock.

"Please" my mother pleaded. "Afterwards we can have ice cream at Serendipity's."

But I didn't want ice cream. I wanted to be back in my room with my Narnia books. Although I knew I was too old to still be reading *The Lion, The Witch and The Wardrobe*, I was always comforted knowing there could be another kingdom where I could escape.

The saleslady, whose name we learned was Florence from a black label on her red jacket, returned with a heap of bras in her arms. I winced as she hung each one on a hook. These bras could have been twisted hangers. I craved lace, flowers, anything pretty.

"Let me just check her size," Florence told my mother and suddenly she grabbed my right breast, weighing it in the powdery creases of her hand as if testing a grapefruit. "Yes," she said, nodding. "I think this is the right size—B."

Face steaming, I tried to hide behind a veil of white tissue paper, which nestled the bra like a precious present. Florence instructed me to bend to my waist, my breasts hanging like half-inflated balloons. The bra itched me the same way as the black wool tights I wore to school. What I saw in the mirror: two Styrofoam cones.

My mother wiped at her eyes. "This is how I'll feel at your wedding," she told me as she opened her purse to find a Kleenex. The saleslady's fingers pushed and pulled the bra with maroon painted claw-like nails. If these were what breasts were for, I didn't want them.

I unhooked the contraption, threw it on the floor, and hugged my old undershirt. "Leave me alone," I shouted, and even the dressing room curtains seemed to shiver.

"I'm sorry," my mother told Florence, which infuriated me, since I wanted my mother to be apologizing to me for this humiliation. "Why don't I find you something you like," my mother said as she parted the red curtains.

That was my cue. I grabbed my sweater, my coat, and ran out of the dressing room. The escalator was only six feet away. I ran down each step, as women with shopping bags made annoying noises but still stepped aside. The sun on Fifth Avenue blinded me and I wasn't sure which way was home. I watched the doorman whistle for a yellow taxi for a woman staggering with brightly wrapped packages. For all I knew my mother could still be looking for the right bra. If this meant becoming a woman, I didn't want anything to do with it.

I felt a hand on my right shoulder. I turned around and there was my mother. She must have been running to find me because she gulped a few times to catch her breath. "Don't worry about it, darling," my mother said. "We can still get ice cream at Serendipity's."

Later that day my mother called the headmaster and said that male teachers checking the female students' backs for brassieres was illegal. Teenage girls' brassieres had nothing to do with education. If he didn't cease with this nonsense, she would contact a lawyer. My father stopped playing bridge with him. A year later the headmaster died of a heart attack right in the middle of the holiday assembly. Only a few teachers shed a tear as they wheeled his body out of the auditorium. All my friends were wearing bras then. My new friend Pauline took me to a boutique on Columbus Avenue owned by her aunt from Paris. All the bras were so beautiful—almost like sugar-spun confections. They were very expensive too, but my mother had given me a hundred-dollar bill. Pauline's aunt, a tall skinny woman who wore tight jeans and Frye boots, encouraged me to buy a red bra. A bra that was the same color as a Valentine hearts box of candy. I didn't show my mother the bra when I came home but she could tell by looking at my chest that something had changed. And something had changed too. Josh Heller, a boy who had ignored me all year, asked me if I would study for our English class in the library. There in the stacks, by the encyclopedias, he kissed me. I pushed his hand away from my chest—he didn't earn that right yet. But I knew I wasn't in Narnia anymore.

PRINCE HAL

There is a thirty-four-story tall condominium on 79th Street and Columbus Avenue that my friend Harry told me would one day collapse into a heap. The condo was constructed in 1983, the tallest building on the block with 165 apartments. "Carbuncle Construction," Harry called it, and it was a true eyesore nestled next to townhouses and brownstones. Across the street was The American Museum of Natural History. And that grand edifice, built in 1869, seemed to sneer at the new intruder with burnished windows that reflected the autumn sunshine with gold antique hues.

"How are you so sure?" I asked Harry that day, who had a sly smile as if he looked forward to the destruction.

"My roommate is sleeping with the architect, who told him that all the engineering designs were miscalculated."

Harry was chuckling, but I was secretly horrified. I could imagine that high-rise toppling over like a set of blocks pushed over by an angry toddler. What would happen to all the families who lived there?

We had just seen a set of adorable twins being led by their adoring parents into the lobby.

"Can't he tell someone?" I asked, my voice rising in panic. "Call *The New York Times*? Notify the mayor?"

"Are you kidding me? That architect would never work again. Come on, Lady Jane, let's go to Hallucination Hall.

Harry was referring to The Hayden Planetarium. The Hayden was known as this name because during their late-night shows that featured rock music, almost all of the audience were high on acid. Their special "Dark Side of the Moon" production, with music by Pink Floyd, was always scheduled after 10 PM to discourage young kids from attending. Harry opened his mouth so I could see the white tab that dissolved on his very pink tongue. I was scared of LSD, and lied to him that I had to write an essay the next morning about Eugene O'Neil's *Clarissa* for my American Theater class.

The lights dimmed and I had a vision of everyone in the audience drifting upwards toward the domed sky, to the illuminated universe. Digital animations spun and sparkled and soared through simulated space. Planets throbbed back and forth in front of me like a swinging face of a clock. I'm sure there were other songs from Pink Floyd, but the really trippy "Us and Them" must have played at least ten times. I would hear that song in my sleep for the following month. When I glanced at Harry, whose face was bathed in green and purple lights, his fixed, drugged grin scared me. Where was he? Certainly not sitting next to me at the Hayden Planetarium. I suddenly took his hand and placed it on my lap. We had been inseparable for six months—it was time. His hand lay limp like a forgotten napkin. He was so stoned he probably didn't realize what I just did. When the show was over, his hand left me in order to furiously applaud.

Harry was still high when we left the show and suddenly realized that he too had an English paper to write about *Tristam Shandy*. "Although perhaps it's better to be stoned to really understand that book," he said as we entered a local diner. Whenever Harry was high or drunk, he had to eat eggs over easy with rye toast and butter, bacon so crisp that it could "cut through metal" and two cups of black coffee. On the Upper West Side in the 1980s, there were Greek diners everywhere, usually named Olympia or Mykonos, with waiters with pasty white skin and black greased black hair who seemed to never sleep. I love these diners as much as Harry, who said the closest thing to a diner in his hometown in Kansas was a Denny's run by high school juniors.

"What did you see when you were tripping?" I asked Harry.

"My missing black bomber jacket. Instead of the planets, it was floating up there in the stars."

Harry still hadn't recovered from the loss of his favorite leather jacket. When he and his family arrived, driving all the way from Kansas to Morningside Heights, they parked their van on Amsterdam Avenue and 120th Street and forgot to lock the doors. After checking out Harry's dormitory, they returned to find their car gone. "Twenty minutes, that's all." All of Harry's suitcases were stolen, along with his records and typewriter. That's how I met Harry. I was walking to my own dorm on Amsterdam when I saw a tall blonde boy who looked my age, with his middle-aged parents staring at a vacant spot on the street. His mother, a chubby woman wearing a bright red puffy jacket, was sitting there on the pavement, openly sobbing.

"What happened?" I asked Harry. "Was she attacked?"

I was a sophomore and knew that this was not a neighborhood to leave an unparked car, much less a van with a license plate from Kansas.

"I guess someone needed some stuff," Harry told me. "Anyway, it's a good excuse to buy new clothes."

I introduced myself to Harry and his parents, and his mother brightened when she saw her son talking to me. "Don't worry about me," she said, finally standing up. "We need to find the nearest police station.

I accompanied Harry and his family to the nearest precinct where we spent three hours waiting to speak to an officer. That's how Harry and I bonded. He told me he was the first in his family to attend college. His parents, who owned a farm, didn't want him to travel to the big bad city. And after what happened to their car, their suspicions could be justified. But this is where Harry belonged. As long as he could remember, he watched every film set in New York City. The grittier, the better. *The Taking of Pelham 123* was probably his favorite.

Harry was glad to be rid of his Kansas clothes, but he did desperately miss his leather bomber jacket his younger sister had bought him as a farewell present. According to Harry, the jacket made him look like Joe Strummer of The Clash. Even with a black leather jacket, there was no way Harry could look like Joe Strummer. He had curly golden hair, freckles, and bright green eyes. He looked like a Kansas farmer's son.

Now, six months later, there in that Greek diner, he was still grieving for that jacket. I reminded him that he could probably find one for resale at Screaming Mimi's down in the East Village.

"But it won't be the same," Harry said, and then ordered a round of eggs and bacon.

"I like a hungry man," the middle-aged waitress with the thick black eyeliner said, winking at him.

"Me too," Harry answered. Waitresses were always flirting with him. I was jealous, and also jealous that no matter what he ate, he never gained a pound.

"I don't know why Greek diner eggs taste different," he said. "I think there's some of that NYC ash that mixes in with them in the kitchen."

"How do eggs in Kansas taste?"

"Like margarine. Everything in Kansas tastes like margarine. Even the people smell like margarine."

He really hated his home state. In high school, Harry was constantly bullied, called a fairy because he liked to read *Jane Eyre*, and was once stuffed into a gym locker and left there for five hours until the school janitor saved him.

"Onward we must flee, Lady Jane," he said after he finished his third cup of coffee. His eyes no longer had that stoned, glazed candy look. "The Smith-Corona beckons uptown."

Although my real name is Janet, Harry always called me Lady Jane because he said I had a regal profile. ("You mean I have a big nose," I told him. "No, regal," he corrected. I, in turn, called him Prince Hal. We were English majors, after all.)

I always believe that a few special people who possess some sort of interior magnets draw you to them. It's only happened to me a few times with people, and Harry was the first. We both loved coffee from Chock Full of Nuts, Werner Herzog films, (we were both taking German, and really tried not to read the English subtitles), bright red Converse high-top sneakers, raisin bagels, punk rock bands that played at CBGB, and Kate Bush's paean to

Wuthering Heights with me making Harry listen to her sing over and over "Heathcliff, it's me, I'm Cathy I've come home," a hundred times. I was also a terrible typist, and many a night Harry agreed to type my endless papers about endless English novels like *Clarissa* and *Tom Jones*. I had decided against Harry's advice, to plunge fully into a class where I had to read a novel—over 500 pages a week. In return, I did Harry's laundry for him. He told me he was allergic to washing machines, and would remain in his filthy clothes forever if I didn't haul the load downstairs to the basement.

In 1980 Columbia University was still all men. Some, not all professors, allowed Barnard women to take classes. I petitioned for a class about Ulysses that Harry was attending, and the professor hated me. He would ignore my raised hand and never personally grade any of the Barnard student papers, but have his Teaching Assistants read them. Joe called him Goebbels and one day, when my hand was wildly waving to make a point about Molly Bloom, the professor called on Harry (who seemed to be asleep) instead. Harry lifted his head and said, "You really are terrified of women, aren't you?"

"Excuse me, Mr..." The professor looked down at his class list for Harry's last name.

"It's Osmond," Harry lied. His last name was Harrigan. Harry Harrigan. "I should have been a circus star," he always said. To my growing embarrassment, Harry stood up and pointed to me.

"Why do you continue to ignore my academic colleague her? Does she threaten you? How the hell can any of us men talk about Molly Bloom? Joyce barely comprehended her. Don't you think a woman has something to say that no one of us could ever understand?"

My face was burning. When I stumbled out of the classroom, Harry left too and followed me.

"What did I do wrong?" he asked, his hands raised as if arrested.

"I can defend myself," I told him. "I don't need a man to save me."

"Thanks," Harry said, his own face now flushing. "That's really nice of you. I could get a *D* on my paper because Goebbels is pissed at me. Last time I defend you, my dear."

"I don't need defending!" I screamed, and then ran down the hall, nearly falling down the stairs that lead to the exit.

That was our first argument. I returned to my dorm room, yelled at my roommate who was playing Elton John too loudly, slammed the door and started weeping. I was in love with Harry. There were other boys who attracted me but no one "got me" the way Harry did. I knew he didn't love me. How can I change his mind? Or maybe I should just forget him. He was now hanging out with a pretentious crowd who met every night at The Marlin bar on Broadway and 110th Street, a bar so filled with smoke that you could barely see the person sitting next to you. His friends all hung out at downtown clubs and knew Warhol and bought their clothes at cool vintage clothing stores and had second homes in places I never heard of like Martinique or Belize. I don't know why Harry liked them. They certainly didn't like me. Whenever I joined them, I felt a coolness in the room, as if someone had opened a window. In a way, it was very much like being back in that Columbia classroom.

After that argument, I stayed away from Harry. I would occasionally pass him on campus and he would look at me, stop, but I would continue walking. I couldn't sleep at night and was skipping meals in order to study, especially Ulysses. Professor Goebbels was finally taking notice of me. My last paper received an *A*-. An *A* would have been impossible.

One night, about three months since our fight, when I returned home, Harry was in my kitchen, talking to my roommate Gretchen. "Hi," he said. In his hands were two tickets. "Get your coat now," he said, walking to the door.

"Where are we going?" I asked.

"I have two tickets to see The Talking Heads. Front row seats."

He knew I loved David Byrne. I had discovered The Talking Heads in high school while Harry had to listen to their records in his childhood bedroom that he shared with his six-year-old brother. They were now playing at Forest Hills Stadium.

"Thank you," I told him. "And you can call me Lady Jane. I miss being royal."

"Me too," he told me. "I tried to teach my cat to say Prince Hal, but he only spit out a fur ball."

That concert was magical. Both Harry and I sang along to every lyric. I had seen Talking Heads up close at CGBG, but being in the first row of a large concert was a completely different experience. It was as if I were royal.

On the subway back we both sang "Psycho Killer" at the top of our lungs and a few people moved away. We decided to have a beer at The West End, and I was glad Harry didn't insist on his hangout at The Marlin. The bartender who seemed to know Harry gave us free tequila shots along with our beers. I didn't realize I was drunk until I slipped off my stool and landed hard on the ground. Harry laughed as he picked me up.

"Hey, lightweight," he said.

"I have a huge crush on David Byrne," I told him.

"Me too," Harry answered.

"I mean, I could have sex with him right now."

"Me too," Harry said softly.

I didn't get it at first.

"What?" I asked.

Harry looked at me and shook his head. "Go ahead, Lady Jane, finish your beer. I have something to tell you."

I should have known. I wasn't a country hick. I knew several gay boys when in high school. But I wasn't in love with them. I was in love with Harry.

Harry picked up his beer and took three deep sips and then wiped the foam from his lips. "I like men," he said. "I mean, I only like men."

The jigsaw pieces fell into place. Why he never looked twice at me when he wandered into my room and saw me in my bra and underwear. All those nights at the cinema when I snuggled close to him and he never placed his arm around me. The time I placed his hand on my crotch.

"Well I get Byrne first," I said. We stared at each other and then both started laughing.

I wasn't shocked but disappointed.

Harry leaned over and placed his mouth over my ear. "I'm sleeping with that bartender," he told me. I turned around and saw that the bartender, who was about six feet two with a shaved head and an earring, was staring at us.

"Really?" I asked.

"Cross my heart and hope to die. But whatever you do, Lady Jane, please don't tell my Mama."

When we walked back to my dorm that night, his arm was finally around my shoulders.

"You're not mad at me, are you?" he asked, his voice suddenly soft and unsure.

"Of course not. Not mad, but I am allowed to be sad. I thought I was in love with you."

"Yeah, I thought I was in love with you too. My feelings have always been mixed up about men and women. But then I met Mitch."

"Mitch, is that the bartender's name?"

Harry nodded and his eyes looked shiny. "With Mitch, I knew for sure."

"Friends?" I asked, shaking his hand.

"More than friends. But not lovers. We're in a weird part of the galaxy, Lady Jane."

He dropped his hand and touched my face. I stared deep into his eyes and then turned away, trying to hide my tears.

Harry watched me enter my dorm, show my ID card to the security guard and stand by the elevator. He was still there when the elevator door opened. Alone in the car, I let myself weep fully for a minute and then wiped my eyes. "Mitch," I said out loud trying out my best Debbie Harry voice. "You better treat him right or one way or another I'll get ya, get ya, get ya!"

Harry and I remained friends, although we were in different crowds. Now openly out, Harry spent time with a group of young men who were not as pretentious as his crowd at The Marlin. To my surprise, he became sober. Mitch, the bartender, told him he drank too much. Harry had dyed his hair bleached blonde and now wore ripped jeans and torn t-shirts, a true punk rocker. He told me he was not going back to Kansas for Christmas. "This Dorothy doesn't believe there is no place like home." He had told his younger brother he was gay, and now his parents wanted to send him to a Christian conversion camp.

"What's that?" I asked.

"It's a horror show. We had a boy in our class sent to one in West Virginia, and the first night he came home he set himself on fire and jumped off the roof of his house."

I became involved in the campus theater group and started writing plays. Harry was a fierce critic, but I knew he was honest. "No one talks like that in a dole queue in London," he once told me about a one-act play. "Have you even been in a dole queue, Lady Jane?"

I fell in love with one of my actors, who was supposed to be Pre-Med and had infuriated his parents by applying instead to Julliard. We both went to London for our Junior Year Abroad and promptly broke up the first week there. I wasn't bothered. There were so many English actors to fall in love with in London. I wrote long letters to Harry about how claustrophobic I felt in the Tube stations, and that a play I saw in a pub about Rosencrantz and Guildenstern was the most exciting new theater I had ever seen. Harry never wrote back but I wasn't mad. He would tell me about his life when I returned to New York.

I had hoped to see Harry when I returned, but when I telephoned, he told me he couldn't see me. "Something's up," he said. "Maybe next week."

He sounded very tired. On my way to Chock Full of Nuts, I ran into my old roommate. "Have you heard about Harry?" she asked me.

"No, what?"

"He has that gay kind of cancer."

In London, I had known about AIDS, but didn't pay much attention since I was always either writing plays or attending the theater. Harry still wasn't returning my phone calls. He no longer lived in this dorm and when I went to the registrar the woman behind the desk told me Harry Harrington had withdrawn from the semester. The only place I could go was the West End. To my relief, Mitch was still there.

"He's in Buenos Aires," Mitch told me. "He has a new boyfriend. Supposedly there's a new kind of treatment there."

I stared at Mitch who looked healthy and sturdy. "You're fine?" I asked.

"So far. I'm lucky. But who knows?" He turned around and began serving his customers. His shoulders were shaking, and I knew that Harry had broken his heart.

I was accepted into graduate school in Boston, and for two years had no contact with Harry. But I knew about this horrendous plague that was destroying so many men, and several students in my own program withdrew to be with their families when they were sick. I knew Harry could not return home. If he still was in Argentina, perhaps was happy and even cured.

I was fortunate enough to have a play produced off-off Broadway when I was twenty-three. To my absolute surprise, Harry was there opening night. He was alone. The boy I knew was now a man. The disease had made most of his hair fall out, and he walked into the theater with a cane. His face was white. It was as if all the freckles had been wiped away.

"Congratulations, Lady Jane," he told me.

"Please, let me get someone to help you." I took his arm, which felt as brittle and thin as a matchstick. Harry was always skinny, but this was beyond skinny. His face was all bones and sockets.

"Break a leg, babe," he whispered to me.

I had to run backstage to calm the actors. The performance was good for opening night, even though one actor missed a few lines. After the audience had left, Harry still sat in his seat.

"I have a present for you, Lillian Hellman," he told me, leaning down to take out a bottle of champagne from his backpack. "Congratulations. I only have paper cups."

"They're the best kind," I said, sitting next to him.

"I wish I could join you," Harry said. "I don't drink and I'm on meds anyway."

"Are they helping?"

Harry shook his head. I noticed he was wearing a leather coat.

"Nice."

"Not as nice as my leather bomber jacket."

"Didn't you say it made you look a little like Fonzie?"

"Never," Harry declared.

My boyfriend and I had to help him stand up and walk into the lobby. Harry walked so slowly that with each step something squeezed hard in my throat. We would try to help him, but he insisted that he was fine. When we found him a taxi, he said he would take it alone. No matter how much I pleaded, he did not want me to join him. I did not know then that he was living in a group house with other men who had AIDS. I found this out six months later, after he died.

Harry was only twenty-three years old. He never graduated college. He was too young to even know who he wanted to be. What he wanted to do. Life was snatched away so quickly that he couldn't have possibly had the chance to grasp it in his hands. It didn't make sense. But none of it made sense to all those who died.

Mitch told me about Harry's death one night when he was on break from bartending at The West End. Harry eventually returned to Kansas, taking back his oath that he would never go home again. Perhaps the people who were taking care of him had died. Or he wanted to see his siblings and the farm. Mitch said Harry's parents refused to have anyone but close relatives attend the funeral. They told everyone that he had died from pneumonia. When Mitch had written to his parents, they returned his envelope unopened.

After Mitch told me this, I stood so completely still that I thought I stopped breathing. Then I went to my apartment, and ran to my record collection. I still had my record player and played "Psycho Killer" by The Talking Heads at full volume over and over until the walls seemed to shake. Loud knocking started on my door and my doorman rang me from my lobby. My boyfriend found me on the floor, shouting along to the lyrics when I wasn't sobbing.

Almost four decades later, that high-rise condominium on Columbus Avenue and 79th Street still stands. Unlike you, my dear Prince Hal, the edifice did not crumble. Although you hated it, I think of you whenever I stand beneath the awning. Yes, life still exists there. Families leave the lobby with strollers, single men and woman walk their dogs. The doorman nods at me with recognition. You would probably never have chosen this apartment building to be your memorial. But sorry, Harry, this is for me. Maybe I chose to live on the Upper West Side to be near you. I'm here right now, tilting my head all the way past the very top apartment on the thirty-fourth floor. If I crane my neck even farther, I can see the stars in the sky, like the fabricated illumination we saw that night so long ago at The Hayden Planetarium. Maybe you're up there right now, floating in the galaxy, wearing that lost leather bomber jacket and singing "Us and Them." You want to know something, Harry? I prefer my own new title: "Me and You." Better than, "Psycho Killer" right? Me and You, Prince Hal. Always.

BLUE MOON ON RIVERSIDE

At fifteen years old, I was a pyromaniac. I would try to set my hair on fire with the fancy matches my mother collected from Manhattan's finest bars: Lutece, The Carlyle and The Plaza. I would steal them from a back drawer in the kitchen and my mother never noticed.

Right after I returned from my last high school class, I would grab a random book of matches, bring them to my bathroom, and lock the door. No one was ever at home. I would take a deep breath, exhale, and then strike a match.

The orange flames would dance, sway and pulsate. I loved to listen to the unique song of fire: snap, crackle and pop. The scent of sulfur was as intoxicating to me as Joy, my mother's favorite perfume. If my hair caught fire, the smell would change dramatically into something animal.

One by one, I lit a match and brought the flickering fire to my scalp. I loved that moment when it was so close—I could practically hear my hair sizzling. Sometimes the sulfur would tickle the inside of my nose. My hand never trembled. Would my hair burst into flames or just smolder? Would the rest of me become a conflagration?

My bathroom, decorated with thick pink towels from Bloomingdale's, could transform into an inferno that threatened not just my apartment, but also the entire building. That would make me not only a pyromaniac, but an arsonist. A criminal.

It never went that far. I threw the matches into the sink and turned on the faucets. Each burning match would extinguish with a sigh that said, "she lost her nerve again." I would watch the soggy black sticks spin in a pool of water and then be sucked down into the noisy drain. I was jealous of these matches. I wanted to vanish too.

Why was I trying to set my hair on fire?

Maybe it was because my mother's chiropractor felt my boobs when he was supposed to be checking my spine.

When I told my mother she said, "Don't be ridiculous, Hannah. Doctor Carter is the best in his field, and you were lucky to get an appointment."

Or maybe it was because my Spanish teacher, Senor Millones, held up my homework and called my handwriting chicken scrawl and started clucking and waving his arms like a bird right in front of my desk. The class laughed so hard that a few students fell out of their seats. After that, almost everyone in tenth grade called me "Pollo," and when I walked by, they would start squawking like my teacher.

My biology instructor, Mr. Alexander, gave me an F and wrote in big bold red letters: NEXT TIME MAKE SURE YOUR LAB PARTNER IS A BOY.

Or maybe the reason I was playing with matches was because I was obsessed with a sixteen-year-old boy. Jason Brennan. Who didn't love me.

He showed up at my best friend Mary's New Year's Eve party at her parents' apartment on West End Avenue. No one knew who invited him. Jason Brennan, I once heard a boy say. Wasn't his nose once broken? And his mouth is too big? Jason was beautiful because he wasn't perfect. His nose did look as if it had been half smashed a long time ago, but that made him more alluring. Tall and skinny with long limbs that always seemed to get jumbled with each other. Eyes that were green or grey or even blue, depending on the light. His too-large mouth made him look like Mick Jagger. He always wore a denim jacket with one torn sleeve. He could be every rock star that stared down from framed posters on my friends' walls. He didn't go to our school but the Bronx High School of Science, which was several long and confusing subway rides away. To me, the Bronx could have been another continent.

If it wasn't for me being drunk on some cheap cherry brandy, I never would have said a word. Yet he spoke to me as he walked into the hallway.

"Hey," he said to me.

"Hey," I said back, willing my knees not to buckle.

Jason stared at me in a way as if he was trying to remember my name. I licked my lips, hoping that would increase the shine of my lip gloss.

"How did you know about Mary's party?" I asked, trying to keep my voice steady.

"Can't remember," Jason answered with a shrug. He wasn't wearing his usual denim jacket but a sweater that was the color of deep green. His damp hair seemed to be laced with wet snowflakes, and I resisted the urge to push away one recalcitrant lock that hid his left eye.

"I'm…" I began, prepared to tell him my name.

Jason wasn't paying attention to me but to his watch. "Hey, it's almost midnight. I promised my Mom I would call her. Do you know where the phone is?"

"The fur closet," I said.

Mary's parents hid their phone there in order to discourage their three daughters from talking all night to their friends. Mary found it, of course, but it was still a secret.

Jason grinned. "No way," he said. He had dimples too.

"Follow me," I said, taking his hand. No one, not even Mary, had seen him enter the apartment. I was determined to get to that closet, which was a few feet away, as quickly as possible.

I opened the door and we walked into a universe of mink. So many coats! The fur brushed against our faces, and I fought the urge to sneeze. I knocked over a pile umbrellas stored in the corner.

Jason groped for a light switch but couldn't find one. I didn't help him. Darkness was my friend.

Outside the closet, we could hear the partygoers counting down to midnight. "10, 9, 8 7, 6, 5, 4, 3, 2, 1. *Happy 1994!*"

"Auld Lang Syne," I said to Jason, and then he leaned forward and that stray lock of hair fell into my face.

I don't know if I kissed Jason first or if he kissed me, but I tripped over an umbrella and he caught me. Suddenly, we sank deep into the depths of the closet, tangling into each other. My hand was in his hair, his face, his elbow by my shoulders, my mouth discovering his mouth. I was surprised his lips were so soft.

"Happy New Year," he said, stopping to take a breath, and I kissed him again and again.

I could have stayed there forever with Jason Brennan even if it meant lying very uncomfortably against an umbrella.

"Jesus, sorry," said Mary, who stared and then quickly slammed the door, but the spell was broken.

Jason stood up and smoothed his wrinkled sweater with the same hands that had been touching me everywhere.

"Damn, I'm late," he told me, opening the door.

"Another party?" I asked, trying to keep my face, which had been rubbing against his for the last ten minutes, composed.

"No. Not a party," he said, frowning. "Someone I promised to be with tonight."

Then, almost in a whoosh of air, he was gone. Out of the apartment and into the elevator so fast that he looked like a blur. As I heard the elevator close, I realized that he never asked my name.

The rest of the night, Mary and I discussed every second of our encounter. Was I sure he didn't know my name? Maybe, in the heat of passion, he said it and I didn't hear it.

School was still closed for Christmas break and everyone had disappeared. I had nothing to do except call Jason's home. Mary had found his family's number for me. I was calling twice a day. The phone rang and rang—sad, empty sounds.

Was no one ever home? What would I say, anyway? "Hi Jason, this is Hannah Jacobs. We kissed on New Year's Eve. Hope you remember me?"

He had to know my name. I felt like I was vanishing. I could have been a blackboard where all the chalk had faded.

Since I was getting nowhere with the phone calls, Mary came up with a plan. His apartment building, on Riverside Drive on 79th Street, The Lombardy, was only a fifteen-minute walk from my apartment building on Central Park West.

Once school began again for the winter term, I would set my alarm for six in the morning to be sure that I was standing on the corner right outside his apartment building which luckily had only one entrance. When Jason left his lobby for school, I would "accidentally" bump into him. Then I would know if he knew my name and if he remembered our kiss.

What I didn't count on was the weather. Riverside Drive was in another climate zone from the rest of Manhattan. Riverside Drive was known as Siberia. Gales that could knock you over in seconds. I knew someone who had to take a taxi from Broadway to Riverside Drive so her grandmother wouldn't be blown away. Schoolgirls would clutch hands so they wouldn't lose each other. Wind that was like a mugger pushing you on the ground and stomping on every inch of your body. Jason was worth the punishment.

That first morning when I left my apartment building, it was January cold. Not terrible, not murderous, just cold. By the time I reached Riverside Drive, I literally had to hold onto an icy lamppost for support.

At seven in the morning, a very weak sun was trying to rise in the sky. I watched the residents come and go. A short, uniformed doorman wearing a ridiculous large gold braided hat opened the door for them with all his strength against that Riverside Drive gale. There were businessmen, women walking their dogs, and a few kids on their way to the school bus.

My teeth were chattering, my bones were splintering, and I wasn't sure if I had a tongue anymore. I jumped up and down to stay warm. Where was Jason? He should have left for school by now. Winter break was officially over. I had been there for at least fifteen minutes and had my first class in five minutes. The doorman, who was now standing at his post, glared at me with a cold look that made me shiver more. Suddenly, he started rushing toward me. His coat was open, and his black sleeves were flapping about like bat wings.

"Can I help you?" he asked in a funny foreign accent that reminded me of a villainous children's television cartoon character. The doorman was really short—we could look at each other eye level.

"I'm waiting for someone," I answered. The wind made the hair blow all over my face. But that doorman's hat stayed securely on his head.

"You're waiting to be sent to the hospital," the doorman said. His cheeks were flushed with the wind. He looked the same age as my father. His eyes were very dark—the same color as dates.

My teeth were uncontrollably chattering. I couldn't take this wind anymore. The doorman turned to open the door for yet another woman walking a dog. I ran down the block, my chest heaving with what felt like massive ice cubes.

Back at school, I was sneezing so much that they sent me to the school nurse.

"Dear God, Hannah," she said to me, feeling my frozen hands. "Where have you been?"

"Riverside," I told her. The nurse gasped as if just said I shot someone.

Luckily, I didn't have to explain since the bell rang for class. It took me about two hours to thaw. Mary made me drink hot tea after hot tea in the school cafeteria.

"Maybe you should wait until spring," she told me.

I shook my head. "It'll be too late. It's now or never."

That afternoon, however, I didn't feel so encouraged. I took a book of matches, this time from Pete Luger Steakhouse, and headed straight to the bathroom. I lit so many matches that my sink became a bonfire. I leaned into that conflagration and felt my eyebrows singe. Jason Brennan would never love me. Someone that afternoon had stuffed chicken feathers in my locker. My boobs still hurt where that chiropractor squeezed.

If my mother hadn't arrived early from work, who knows what might have happened.

"Hannah," she called out. "Is that smoke?"

I quickly opened the windows and turned on the faucets. When I came into the kitchen, her nose was sniffing.

"Sorry," I said. "Homework. Science experiment."

"Next time, do your homework in the lab. I don't want my home to smell like a chimney. Hannah, is that a pimple on your chin? I should call my dermatologist for you."

No way would I ever see any of my mother's doctors again. But she was right. I did have a pimple on my chin, which I promptly popped in my still smoky bathroom.

The next morning, I was back again on the corner of 79th Street, but better prepared this time with long underwear, four pairs of thick socks, an Icelandic sweater, earmuffs and gloves. But that wind still pushed and pulled and pulverized. This time I clung to a fire hydrant. To my surprise, that little doorman with the big hat saw me and directly walked to my spot.

"You again?" the doorman asked with that funny accent.

"I'm waiting for a friend," I said.

"On this corner? You want to know what frostbite does to a person's fingers?" He took off his left leather glove, and I saw that his hand was missing a pinkie. I gasped. "Lucky it was just one finger," he added.

"Where did that happen?" I asked.

"A place that makes this street feel like Hawaii. You should be in school. What's your name?" the doorman asked.

"Hannah."

Maybe I shouldn't have told him my real name. He could report me to the cops. But I'm glad I did because it changed everything.

"Hannah," he said slowly. Something in his face softened. My name sounded different, with an exotic emphasis on the last syllable. The wind blew me so hard that I lost my grip on the fire hydrant and nearly collapsed into him. The doorman gripped me firmly by the arm.

"You're coming inside. Lobby. Now."

How could I wait in the lobby? There would be no more pretense of "accidentally" running into Jason. The doorman waved his hand with the missing finger. He was right. I didn't want to lose any part of my body.

"I can only stay for a few minutes," I said, following him past the awning and to the front door.

When he opened it for me, I could see that the lobby was lit with large golden lamps and there were big red sofas and upholstered chairs. It looked exactly like my building lobby except the floor was marble.

The doorman pointed to one of these chairs. "Sit," he *commanded*.

If Jason showed up, I could lie and say I was waiting for someone else who lived in the building. Maybe an elderly aunt. The Lombardy was the type of building where elderly aunts lived.

I watched the doorman greet every person in the lobby by name. The old lady with the walker was Mrs. Schwartz. The woman wearing a long down jacket and a polka-dotted hat was named Farrah. I thought only blonde glamourous actresses were named Farrah. Twins wearing matching red snowsuits tumbled out of the elevator and the doorman chased them.

"Milo," they screamed in glee. "Try to catch us!"

So, the doorman's name was Milo.

I glanced at my watch, as if I had plenty of time to kill and I wasn't missing my first period English class. After Milo played with the snowsuit kids, he slowly walked up to me, crossed his arms in front of his chest, and then took out a white handkerchief.

"You're not the first," he said.

"What?" I asked.

"Lots of girls show up for Jason Brennan."

I stood up so suddenly that I was dizzy. Sinking back into the chair, I hoped I had misheard him.

"How do you know I was waiting for Jason Brennan?" I asked.

The doorman offered me his handkerchief. Did he think I was about to cry?

"You must be the sixth girl this year waiting for the superstar."

"The sixth girl?"

The doorman sighed. I could tell he had had this conversation before.

"Look, Hannah. You're what, fifteen, sixteen? In my country, you would already be married. You're young. There will be another boy."

But I didn't want any boy. I wanted Jason.

The elevator opened. An old man with a walker tentatively took a step.

"Give me a moment," the doormen told me. I watched him adjust the scarf on the old man's neck and then help him get into a black car that was waiting outside the awning. When he returned to me, he was blowing on his hands as if he was not wearing gloves.

"You know Ol' Blue Eyes?" he asked.

"Who?"

"Frank Sinatra. My favorite. Every time I see one of you girls, I think of the song *Blue Moon*. The saddest lyrics in the world." The doorman sang softly, his voice echoing in the now empty lobby. *"Blue Moon/You saw me standing alone/Without a dream in my heart. Without a love of my own."*

The song affected Milo more than me and he wiped his eyes with the handkerchief.

"What time does Jason leave for school?" I asked. The doorman's song did not deter me.

Milo must have heard the determination in my voice. He shrugged. I won.

"Jason leaves for swim practice at five. So, I would say you should show up in the afternoon."

"Will you be here?" I asked. In my apartment building, there were at least three doormen who had different shifts.

"I'm always here," Milo said, heading to the front door where a woman with a suitcase waited for him.

At school, Mary pestered me about Jason. I just shook my head, not wanting to confide about Milo. During my library hour, I studied Spanish. I would get an *A* on my next exam. Senor Millones would be the one squawking.

I returned the next day at four. There was a different doorman standing by the door, very tall and skinny. I was heartbroken. I turned around and there was Milo, walking down the block, holding a Styrofoam cup with gloved hands. He nodded at me.

"Have you seen Jason?" I asked.

"Not yet. Maybe I missed him during my break. He'll show up." Milo blew on the top of his coffee. "You sticking around?"

I was sticking around all right. The wind pushed both of us into the lobby and I sat down in the same red upholstered chair. No one seemed to notice a teenage girl with a backpack in the lobby. There were many girls who looked just like me in that family building.

That January afternoon began my month with Milo. He loved to talk, and I was his audience. When he was in high school, he wanted to be a chemist. Although he was now a doorman, it was like the same job. Handling all these people in the building was like experimenting with the different elements in his lab. You never knew what would happen when all these ingredients were mixed. Mrs. Schwartz of 5B couldn't stand to be in the elevator with Mrs. Levin of 6A. Mr. McCarter of 12D hated dogs, which drove Mrs. Rivera crazy since she had three poodles and a Lab.

"What about Jason's parents?" I asked. I was growing bored about hearing about all the other residents.

"My favorite people. Mrs. Brennan..." He stopped, bit his lip and looked away. "A true gem."

That's all the information he would offer about the Brennan family. I was getting frustrated that I never once saw Jason. When I asked Milo, he always had the same reply. "Patience is a virtue. My favorite English expression."

When he wasn't too busy with his doorman duties, he'd tell me about his life. Milo lived in a building filled with families from all over the world. "The United Nations of Queens." He met many friends at an ESL class. But Milo was way ahead of them.

"Still, there are some things that confuse me," he said, opening up a folded piece of paper in his uniform pocket and pointing to a phrase. "This expression—What am I, chopped liver? What does that mean? Is chopped liver bad?"

"I never tasted it," I told him.

"What's happening?" Mary asked me each night on the telephone. "Operation Brennan is so stalled."

"He'll show up," I said, thinking of Milo's promise.

Mary did some reconnaissance work with her cousin at the Bronx High School of Science. Jason was not in class. No one had seen him since January. Since I was hanging out in his building, I needed to find out about his mysterious disappearance.

That next afternoon, I didn't waste any time. "Where is Jason?" I asked Milo. "No one has seen him for at least two weeks."

"Oh, he's around," Milo answered. He was sorting through a pile of packages and didn't look at me.

The tall and skinny doorman opened the door that led to the basement and began speaking to Milo in a foreign language. This doorman scared me. He had a scar on his face, thick eyebrows, and never smiled.

"Milo, where are you from?" I asked him after the doorman left. It surprised me he had never told me before.

"Queens, New York."

"No, really."

"A place that doesn't exist anymore," Milo said quietly. I would learn not to pursue it any further. Milo had a dark side. Sometimes he would sink into a deep silence that I knew not to disturb.

My parents asked about my grades and nothing else. I told Milo about my Spanish teacher making fun of my handwriting and he said that if I were his daughter, he would wait for that teacher after school and teach him a lesson. I told him how my biology teacher wanted the girls to have male lab partners since only boys understand science.

"Didn't this idiot ever hear of Madame Curie?" Milo asked.

Mary was still confused about what was going on at The Lombardy. She even wanted to join me, but I emphatically said no.

"But what do you, just wait?" she asked.

"Yeah, I just wait." Which was not exactly a lie.

Sometimes, during his break, Milo would help me with my biology homework. I wrote on top of my test WITHOUT THE HELP OF A BOY. When Mr. Alexander returned the test to me, with 100 circled in red ink, he smiled and whispered, "touché."

"Congratulations," Milo said when I told him my news. He shook my hand. I looked again at the missing pinky.

"Milo, where is your pinky?"

"Left it in a field very far away. Probably some bird's breakfast."

Milo certainly intrigued me, but I couldn't wait in the lobby forever. There had been no news about anyone seeing Jason for the last two weeks. Whenever I asked Milo about Jason he would shrug and say again, "patience is a virtue."

One Monday there was a major announcement at my school. Senor Millones had taken a leave of absence. A new Spanish teacher, Senorita Lopez, was his replacement.

I ran to The Lombardy that day, curious if Milo had indeed threatened my teacher. When I arrived, nearly breathless from my sprint, I didn't see Milo, but instead, the tall doorman with the scar. I felt brave. Maybe this doorman could give me more information.

"Is Jason Brennan home?" I asked.

The doorman didn't answer and looked past his shoulder.

"Why do you want to know?"

"I'm his cousin."

"If you're his cousin, then you know he's not here."

"Not here?" I couldn't be sure if I heard right since he had a thicker accent than Milo.

"Whole family gone. Since January third. Excuse me."

The doorman went inside. I stood there by the building, my body shaking as if being battered by Riverside's most ferocious storm. When Milo appeared, sipping coffee from his Styrofoam cup, I startled him so much that the coffee spilled all over his uniform.

"Hey!" he shouted, trying to mop up the liquid with his handkerchief.

"You lied to me. About Jason. He was never here!"

"Come inside, Hannah. Too cold here."

I noticed his eyes refused to meet my own.

'No," I said loudly. "I want to know the truth."

"The truth?" Milo walked over to a nearby garbage can and tossed out his coffee cup. When he returned, he seemed like a different man. His body seemed broken, as if the Riverside wind had finally beat him.

"Why did I hang out here day after day, waiting for Jason?"

Milo looked at me. His eyes were streaming with water. I didn't know if they were tears from the cold or somewhere else.

"I am sorry, Hannah," he said in a voice that quavered. "I am selfish. I am thinking of her."

Her? What was he talking about? I was so angry that I could feel my face burn.

"So, you won't tell me where Jason and his family are?"

Milo shook his head, wiping his bleary eyes with the back of his palm.

"My job is to protect the privacy of the building residents," he told me.

"Thanks a lot for wasting my time."

He stumbled as if I had just punched him.

"Was it a waste of your time, Hannah?"

"Absolutely. God, I feel so stupid!" I shouted.

I walked away without looking back. In my apartment, I headed directly into my mother's drawer of matches and chose one from The Rainbow Room. I opened the book and counted all of the matches. Twenty. I could burn so much. Then I heard Milo's sad voice, asking me if he had been a waste of my time. Even though I was still furious, I didn't want to hurt him. Staring at that match book, I realized I didn't want to hurt myself either.

Later that night my father told me that my grandmother in Miami had just had a heart attack. We were all leaving tomorrow morning to visit her. The news was too much for me that day. When my father saw me sobbing, he told me my grandmother would be fine and we would enjoy the Florida sun.

My father was right. My grandmother was fine, and I loved sitting on the beach, feeling the warm rays. It was hard to remember that in New York, it was still winter. My parents decided to stay a week and I could miss school. On the last night in Miami, I called Mary.

"I've been trying to find you," she exclaimed. "I have big news!"

Mary, my diligent detective, discovered what had happened with The Brennan family. Someone's cousin, whose father was a headmaster at a private school in Dallas, told his son that to be kind to a new tenth-grade boy from New York City who would be enrolling in January. His father explained that the boy's mother had cancer and was being treated at a famous hospital in Dallas. She was obsessed with privacy and hated pity. Only her immediate family knew.

At first the cousin said the new boy's name was Josh. Then he realized his mistake. Jason Brennan was the correct name.

I remember Jason at the New Year's Eve party asking to use the phone so he could call his mother. That was the reason he had to leave so quickly.

I wanted to tell Milo that I knew why Jason wasn't there. When I returned in to Riverside Drive in February, there was a warm spell. The temperature was almost forty-five degrees. There was no punishing wind. And no Milo.

"He is gone," the tall doorman said. His accent was stronger than Milo's and I wasn't sure if I understood him correctly.

"Gone?" I asked. "Where did he go?"

"Bosnia. Finding his family."

"Finding?" I wondered if this conversation was so confusing because of the language barrier. The doorman shook his head.

"No, that is the wrong word. Identifying. Milo does not talk of war. You should leave, little girl."

He waved his hand dismissively. I turned around and ran away from the building, fighting tears. That doorman was right. He might as well have said stupid little girl. I knew nothing.

Later that night, I asked my father about the Bosnian War. When he asked why, I lied and said my history teacher had mentioned it in class and I wanted to learn more.

"It's a terrible war, Hannah," he told me. "Once the country was Yugoslavia. Then it was broken into several different parts, often divided by religion The conflict is among people who were once neighbors. Now Muslim families being forced to move or are victims of ethnic cleaning."

My father saw the confusion in my face.

"Genocide."

I knew what genocide meant. We were Jewish. My grandparents had barely escaped Nazi Germany when they were children.

"So many families have disappeared. And what they do to the women..."

My mother gave my father a warning glance. My father pushed away his plate. "I can't eat," he told my mother, as he stood up and went into his study.

The next day I returned to The Lombardy. I wanted to tell the Bosnian doorman that I was sorry what had happened to his country. If he had heard from Milo. If he had found his family alive.

I also wanted to ask the doorman if Milo had a daughter. But he was busy opening the door of a taxicab.

A teenage boy jumped out from the back seat and the first thing I saw were his long legs. His hair was cut short, and the boy wore a denim jacket with a torn sleeve. Jason Brennan.

He walked with a bounce and a confidence that made me think his mother was better. Outside on the pavement, I could see him through the glass lobby door. He pressed the elevator button impatiently, as if someone upstairs was waiting for him. Suddenly, Jason turned his head to me. His eyes squinted, and he focused on my face. Milo was right—Jason did show up. I saw his lips move. I could have sworn he said my name.

Did I follow Jason into that lobby I knew so well? For a few moments, I was tempted. But I realized I had moved beyond Jason. I had wanted him to say my name because I thought I had vanished. But I was visible even before he returned.

I did not stay. I turned my back to The Lombardy and braced myself against the wind of Riverside Drive.

I never saw Milo again. I visited The Lombardy a few more times, but he was never there. Neither was the skinny doorman. There was a new building superintendent who was Polish, and men from Warsaw replaced all the Bosnian doormen.

At Wollman Rink in Central Park, I met a high school Junior named Adam. We skated every Sunday, and on the first day of spring in March he kissed me and said, "Hannah, you're beautiful."

Milo was right—there were other boys. And patience is a virtue.

So yes, this is still a love story, but a different kind of love story. A love story that a fifteen-year-old girl would never believe. A stranger from another country befriended her and made sure she did not disappear. I stopped playing with matches. I didn't hate myself anymore.

I would later learn about the horrors of that war. The Srebrenica massacre, where over three thousand Muslim men and boys were murdered. About the systematic rape and murder of women and girls. (My father had spared me those details.) What Milo returned to must have been hell.

I also know that families survived. I can only hope that instead of having to identify the bodies of his loved ones, Milo discovered them again, alive and safe. I like to believe that Milo's daughter's name is Hannah. I like to imagine Milo singing his favorite Frank Sinatra songs to her. But not *Blue Moon*. That song is just too sad.

WALK THIS WAY

"Walk This Way" by Aerosmith thundered on the speakers when he saw the girl's plaid skirt crumbled on the floor like a discarded tissue. He realized it was the same Catholic school uniform as his sister's. The fat frat boy grinding and panting wore a white tank top, white shorts and reminded him of a polar bear. All he could see of her were small hands and small shoes. The smallness shocked him. There were four other frat boys swaying in some sort of ragged line. The flashing red beer neon sign lit the room into a hellish inferno.

"Running the train," his frat brother Rob shouted as his beer foamed out of the can. He pushed him aside as he ran into the hallway. There were girls slumped against the walls, girls with gold glitter on their lids, girls with their lashes half-glued with mascara. These were not the sorority girls next door. These were girls who had fake IDS and should have been home.

He returned to the room and said, "Hey, this should stop." But it didn't stop. Bile rose in his throat as the first boy sat up, grunted, and a second boy took his place. He finally saw her face. Lipstick smeared, eyes closed, skin so white it looked almost translucent. A corpse yet not a corpse. A girl probably in middle school, her chest rising and falling so slowly.

Stumbling downstairs, he ran into the fresh fall night, gulping the cold air as if he were drowning. The scent of burning leaves. A Halloween skeleton rattling on someone's door. A police car cruised down the street. All he had to do was wave it down. Shout. But instead his hands stayed stuck in his pockets, like heavy useless weights.

He would forget that night until three decades later, September, when he drove his eldest daughter to college. The car radio played that same song: Steve Tyler hissing, *"Ah, just give me a kiss."* Bile rose in his throat.

He had to pull over because he couldn't stop weeping.

"Daddy, what's wrong?" his daughter asked.

He was grateful his wife was still home with his two younger daughters. What would he confess?

He was an accomplice.

For all he knew, that girl, who was now a woman, was damaged. Or maybe dead.

He wiped his eyes with the back of his hand. Then turned off the radio. Stared at his daughter whose pale face showed fear. She needed to hear his voice.

"Beware of boys."

"Beware of men."

"I am a coward."

But instead, he said, "Just so sad that you're leaving home, honey."

Patting her hand, he turned the car radio on, relieved to find a safer station that only played Mozart.

GREEN LOVE

My father didn't notice that I had spilled catchup all over my school uniform blouse because he was busy examining dollar bills. The coffee shop waiter had returned with our change and my father was frowning. I knew the reason why. The dollars the waiter had returned were faded, wrinkled, one even with a little tear in the corner. *Oh shit*, I thought to myself. I had just turned nine and "shit' was my favorite curse word.

"Excuse me," my father called out to the waiter. I saw people turn around and stare. Although it was Sunday, my father was dressed in a three-piece suit and carried a suitcase. I was wearing my school uniform because I forgot to pack enough clothes from my mother's apartment.

The waiter, mumbling in what I thought was Greek, since the diner was called Athena, my favorite Greek goddess, slowly walked over, his hands tying the strings of his apron.

"That's the correct change," he said to my father.

My father picked up the worst looking dollar in the pile.

"Do you know what this is?"

The waiter gave a half moan. "A dollar. What else?"

"This is an article of sacrament," my father said. "You wouldn't find a priest offering communion with a filthy chalice, would you?"

I looked down at my white sleeve covered with red sauce. Here was my getaway. "Dad," I told him, "I need to go the bathroom."

"Wait one second." My father stared at the waiter who was shaking his head like my father was crazy. When it came to money, my father was crazy.

"Money's money," the waiter told him. "Shall I visit the bank and bring you new dollar bills?"

"That would be very considerate," my father answered. "I want the kind of bills that give you paper cuts."

The waiter started laughing. So did the other waiter behind the counter and also the couple sitting behind me. I knew my father was about to lecture about honoring our national currency and no one respected a decent buck anymore. This obsession was one of the reasons my mother left him for a poor artist from France named Michel. The irony was because he was poor, my father had to support my mother and also her new lover.

I rushed into the bathroom and tried to wash the ketchup off the cuff sleeves. I rubbed hard with soap, but the sleeve still had a pinkish tinge. I would have to buy another shirt.

My father waited outside on Madison Avenue. I had lowered my head as I walked through the coffee shop, convinced the customers and the waiters were still in hysterics.

"Why do you always have to embarrass me?" I asked my father, who was straightening his tie. He was a tall good-looking man whose nose had once been broken in a boxing match when he was in high school.

"Rose, as I told you before, if you don't respect a dollar then you are…"

"Worthless," I said.

"That's my smart girl." My father patted me on my shoulder. We were near the Rockefeller Ice Skating Rink. I could hear the laughter and the whooshing of the skaters nearby.

Neither of us was dressed for ice skating but I desperately wanted to be on that ice, gliding beneath the lighted Christmas tree.

"I want to go skating," I said to my father. "Please."

He must have heard the catch in my voice because his face grew a bit pale and he audibly sighed.

"Sorry, Rose, I totally forgot. I have a meeting at the office."

"The office? But it's Sunday."

"Not in Tokyo. Not in Sydney. My fault. I forgot this was my weekend."

My parents had fought during the custody agreement in court. I was surprised he wanted to see me so much. My father complained it was too expensive to keep battling, so he had me one weekend, while my mother had me the rest of the month. But now she was traveling more to Paris with her new boyfriend, so I was beginning to see my father more frequently.

"Hey." My father stopped at a florist on the corner of the street. "Let's go inside. I know you love flowers."

I didn't really like flowers, but I wasn't going to argue with him. I knew he would ask, "Who doesn't like flowers?" as if I were a criminal. He was always buying plants. His bedroom had hanging plants and potted plants. The room seemed to have a greenish glow. Paz, his housekeeper, hated having to always water them.

The florist shop was small and crammed with so many flowers that I sneezed. I went to a corner filled with green plants. They looked lonely there, small and ignored.

"Why don't you buy this plant?" I pointed to a small green thing stuffed in the corner, as if the owner wanted to hide it. "You can keep it in your office and think of me."

"You're better than a plant," my father said, picking up a large bundle of roses. "A Rose deserves roses."

My father bought me a whole bouquet of roses. He arranged them in a vase in my bedroom, then returned to his office. Paz immediately took a look at my ketchup-stained shirt, told me to take it off, and handed me one of my father's t-shirts to wear as she washed it. "Querida, next time do not forget your suitcase," she said. Paz always called me "querida" which meant *darling* in Spanish. Paz was from Chile, with bright dyed red hair. She told me her family had been persecuted by a terrible dictator named Pinochet who kidnapped babies. She lived in a tiny room in the back of my father's apartment. After my parents' divorce, my father rented a two bedroom on Third Avenue. My mother, after many arguments, still had our large apartment on Riverside Drive that faced the Hudson River.

After she washed my shirt, she started ironing my father's shirts with grim determination. I loved Paz. I wished she would work for my mother, but my mother said we had to be careful with our expenses and she didn't want to share anything or anyone with my father.

I told Paz what happened at the coffee shop with the waiter. "Too bad you can't iron his dollar bills too," I joked. Paz didn't smile.

"Money is made of the same paper you use to wipe your ass," she said and then clamped her hand over her mouth. I was laughing. "Dios Mio! What did I just say? Do not tell your father!"

"But it's funny," I said, imagining Paz ironing a whole row of creased dollar bills.

"No, querida, it is not funny. Green Love is triste."

"Triste. What does that mean?"

"Sad."

That night I had a strange dream. A seemingly endless supply of dollars was floating in the air above my head, almost as if they were injected with helium. I tried to catch the dollars, but they kept slipping out of my grasp.

I returned to my mother that week, who was in a fight with her boyfriend and had taken up smoking. I hated the cigarette fog, and opened every window in the apartment. I reminded her that this week in school was Bring Your Parent Day to discuss their jobs. My mother, who had quit modeling and was technically jobless, told me to ask my father instead. "He would love that," she said with a crooked smile.

My father was thrilled. I told him to be at my school at 10:00 AM. Mrs. Sheldon, our teacher, had a large sign taped to the blackboard that said WELCOME PARENTS! The first parent was Joe Ryan's father, who was a police detective. Detective Ryan wore this uniform, and I knew several of the boys were disappointed he didn't carry a gun.

"Most of you kids are good," Detective Ryan told us. "But watch out for the bad. The kids who pressure you to make trouble. Just say no."

"Did you ever catch a bank robber?" Alex Bradley asked.

"How about an axe murderer?" my best friend Zoe said.

Detective Ryan sent a searching look toward Mrs. Sheldon.

"Thank you so much. Next, we have Mr. Harrison, Rose's father. Mr. Harrison works on Wall Street."

My father seemed to glide in newly polished shoes and placed his shiny leather briefcase on Mrs. Sheldon's desk. "Great to be here," he said to my teacher. "How you all doing, kids?"

He could not stop grinning. My dad liked being the star of a show. He opened the briefcase and took out several bundles of tightly bound dollars. I could tell since I was in the front seat that these were one-hundred-dollar bills, or Benjamins, as my father called them. The class gasped.

"This is what Wall Street is all about," my father said, pushing the stack of bills across the desk as if they were decks of cards. "Sometimes it goes to the right places. Sometime the wrong. But you have to keep it moving. When it stops, I'm in trouble.

"Can I touch it?" Joey Barton asked.

"Sure," my father answered. "And you don't even have to wash your hands. I keep my money clean."

"Is that like money laundering?" Nina Hopkins asked.

"What is money laundering?" someone from the back row shouted.

"Hey, Mr. Harrison, can I take some of that home?" Ricky Kling said, standing up from his seat.

Now all the kids were standing to get a better view of the money bundles. Mrs. Sheldon's face was pale. She whispered something to my father, who nodded and then began returning the bundles to his briefcase.

"That's all, folks. Back to work. Good luck!"

My father winked at me as he left the classroom. Zoe touched my shoulder.

"What does your father do again, Rose?"

I shook my head. "I'm really not sure," I answered.

I didn't tell my mother what happened in my classroom, but I did tell Paz when I was at my father's the following weekend.

"What's Wall Street?" I asked Paz, who was sorting through a pile of my father's ironed shirts, all bought from Brooks Brothers.

"Ask your father," she told me.

"I don't want to ask him. He'll probably talk and talk and I won't understand a word. Wall Street sounds like a place filled with walls. Just like prison."

"I have been to prison," Paz said, her face bent over the pile of socks. "I am sure your father does not work in a jail."

I didn't see my father until a month later. He was traveling, he told me, finalizing deals. My mother had broken up with her boyfriend but was still smoking French cigarettes. One afternoon on my way to my father's after school, I saw three police cars parked right in front of his building. A group of men were standing by the awning with cameras. When the doorman saw me, he shouted something and waved his hand. Then I saw him. My father in handcuffs. Two policemen, one who didn't look so very different from Joe Ryan's father, lead my father into the car. My father was staring at the ground. I called out his name but he wouldn't turn his head. The men with the camera were shouting at him. The flash from the cameras hurt my eyes. Suddenly, I felt strong arms around me.

"Dios Mio. Do not look, Rose."

Paz held me close against her, but I struggled from her grasp. As the police car sped away, I started running to catch up with the blazing sirens. Of course, the car was too fast for me. I slipped and scraped both knees. They were bleeding and my vision was blurred with tears. Again, I felt Paz's hands on my shoulders. "Querida, come with me. We need to call your mother."

The rest of the day was a haze of phones ringing, my mother sobbing, and Paz, who bathed my bleeding knees with ice water. No one would explain to me what happened except to say my father had made a big mistake. My mother drank straight from the mouth of a red wine bottle.

"Did it just stop?" I asked her.

"What stopped?" my mother asked.

"The bundles."

"What are you talking about, Rose?" she said, waving the bottle so violently that the wine spilled onto the rug.

The following morning, nursing a hangover with an ice cube pressed against her temple, my mother explained that my father had been involved in a "Ponzi" scheme. I thought she said "Pizza" instead and when I asked again, she said she had a headache.

A few weeks later I was allowed to visit my father's apartment to pick up a few belongings that I had left in my room. The man who answered the door wore a suit just like my father and did not smile at me. I wished Paz were there instead. When I had asked my mother if she could now hire her, my mother told me that Paz had returned to Chile, which I was sure was a lie.

After I collected a few shirts and two books, I walked past my father's office. His plants were still there. I walked inside and turned on the light. Several plants were dead already, their leaves cracked and crumpled. But one small plant, one that reminded me of the lonely plant I had seen at the florist with my father, was still half alive. I ran into my father's kitchen and grabbed the biggest glass I could find. The man in the suit was talking to someone on the phone and ignored me. I brought the glass to the bathroom faucet and filled it to the brim with water. The dry soil of that plant soaked up the water so fast that I quickly returned to the faucet and refilled the glass again. Was it my imagination or did the yellow leaves begin to turn green again? The other plants suddenly seemed to lean toward me, as if they too wanted water. I spent thirty minutes watering even the ones that looked dead, desperately hoping to bring them back to life.

DIRECTIONS

Sofia folded the fitted sheet exactly the way her employer, Mrs. Johnson, insisted, with the top two corners inside out and the elastic edge facing her. Her employer was very adamant about how Sofia laundered, and also how she ironed, cleaned the toilets and used copious amounts of boric acid to kill cockroaches. Sofia didn't mind her employer's directions. They were concise and clear, in a city that often confused her.

At eight in the morning the laundry room was empty, yet the smell of bleach and laundry detergent were still overpowering. The apartment building was half empty because of the Christmas school break.

Sofia enjoyed the quiet because there were no people to share the elevator with her and the large laundry basket. There was one flickering light bulb that still needed to be fixed but Sofia found the whirl of the washing machine, the clothes floating through the dryer and the cranking heat of the radiator to be comforting. Focusing on folding another pile of white sheets somewhat eased the ache in her chest, even though her eyes couldn't help but stare at the clock on the wall. At fifty-nine she was a stout woman with arthritic knees. If she were younger, or even in better health, she would do what must be done. But she didn't trust her body or even her courage.

Hana was an hour late. Her plane from Vienna was due to arrive at six that morning. Sofia gave her strict orders to take a taxi straight from Kennedy to the Upper West Side building, but Hana's journey had begun in Dubrovnik so there may have been delays or cancellations. Hana was told not to carry a cell phone so there was no way to communicate with her. Sofia had never even met her niece. She left Sarajevo in 1985, years before Hana was born.

There was a small shelf in the laundry room filled with donated books from the other apartment residents. To take her mind off the clock, Sofia examined several of these books, mostly paperback mysteries and sports biographies. One shelf contained a series of travel guides. Sofia had never visited London, Paris or Rome. How different her life would have been if she had been born in one of these cities.

A sound on the staircase. For a moment she was frozen, a mildewing paperback about Germany in her hand. Slowly Sofia stepped toward the door. "Hello," she said. No answer. Upstairs she heard the voice of Nick the morning doorman and then a dog barking. The Johnsons had a dog, a poodle named Clarissa who seemed to Sofia to be more like a stuffed animal than a living creature. The Serbian soldiers had murdered her family's dogs for really no other reason than to show that they could. So long ago that she had forgotten the dogs' names but not their corpses, strewn across the doorstep like bloodied fur coats.

She was lucky that Nick, too, was from her country. He knew that Sofia was expecting a visitor and to send Hana immediately to the basement.

One dryer stopped with a sharp click. As Sofia began to open it, she heard footsteps. Whirling around, she saw a tall figure with bright blonde hair wearing a black leather jacket and high dark boots. She did not expect anyone in her family to be so fair.

"Tetka, ovdja sam," the girl said softly, standing uncertainly outside the door.

"Only English," Sofia told her. "Only English, do you understand?" She did not intend to sound so harsh, but she must transform this Sarajevo girl into an American. Sofia noticed immediately the cheap looking stone-washed jeans, the shiny fake leather jacket and the harsh makeup, particularly the shade of red lipstick that screamed Eastern European.

"I am here," the girl said, smiling. Her teeth were crooked—another sign that she was not American.

"You are late." Sofia heard that her voice was too harsh and flat.

"A snowstorm in Vienna." Hana walked into the room, rubbing her eyes. "The plane too crowded. I could not sleep."

"Welcome to the United States." Sofia's hand plunged into her apron pocket in order to find a tissue. "Come here."

Hana lifted her arms expecting an embrace. When Sofia took the tissue and roughly wiped the lipstick off her mouth, Hana jumped back in surprise.

"You must look like an American girl," Sofia told her. "Someone may follow you. No one must recognize you as a girl from Bosnia. Here, look in that shopping bag in the corner. What's in there belongs to you."

Hana followed Sofia's pointed finger to a brown paper bag on the floor beneath an ironing board. Leaning over, she took out a sweatshirt with the logo Columbia University and a New York Yankees baseball hat.

"Take off that jacket. I didn't know they still made such cheap trash. The sweatshirt should fit you. The hat too."

Hana silently obeyed her. Sofia knew that she was trained to follow directions and not to ask questions. Now, with the lipstick gone and wearing the new sweatshirt and hat, Hana could resemble any of the young girls Sofia had seen on the Broadway subway commuting to Morningside Heights.

"Better?" Hana asked.

"Much better. Here is the backpack. It is also from Columbia University." Sofia gently lifted the blue backpack that had been hidden beneath a pile of dirty clothes. Hana accepted it, slowly placing a strap around each slender shoulder.

"It is heavy," she said, adjusting the backpack's straps.

"That is the right size." Nick told her the gun was one of the best for the purpose. Sofia hated touching the cold metal and Nick laughed, saying his youngest niece at nine, could shoot better than anyone else in his family.

"Silencer, yes?" Hana asked. She stood straighter now, her mouth and face pale, trying not to be a girl but a soldier.

"Of course. You know how to use it, right?"

Directions

Hana rolled her eyes and looked suddenly so much younger. They told Sofia she was twenty-three, but Sofia wondered now if they lied about her age.

"Yes, Tetka, they trained me well."

She had forgotten not to use her own language, but Sofia held her tongue. "Come here," Sofia told her, as Hana walked over to a white round plastic table. Nick also gave her a subway map, which was spread out, unfolded with a few creases. "You must listen carefully to my directions. We will begin with square one."

Hana frowned. Her eyes were a light blue, the color of Mr. Johnson's favorite dress cotton shirts. No one in Sofia's family had blue eyes.

"What is square one?" Hana asked.

"I thought you knew English," Sofia snapped. "Square one means the beginning. Nothing can go wrong here. In one minute, you'll open that door, walk up the stairs and go through the garbage room. That is square one. Be careful you don't trip over the garbage bags outside. Even in this fancy neighborhood, the Sanitation Department takes their time."

"Sanitation department?"

"People who pick up the trash." A warm wave of irritation flushed Sofia's face. What was wrong with her, talking about the sanitation department? Hana must act quickly since she had a flight back to Dubrovnik tonight. Sofia placed her forefinger on the MTA map and tapped loudly to be sure Hana was watching. "When you leave through the lobby, you will walk four blocks to 96th Street. There, you will take a right and walk three blocks to Broadway. You will see a sign for the subway with the numbers, 1, 2 and 3. I will give you a MetroCard. You will pass it through the turnstile and go to the downtown station. Walk slowly but steady. The numbers 2 and 3 are the quickest to Times Square, but you can also take the number 1. Are you following me?"

"Yes," Hana answered and there was a new stillness to her voice that made Sofia realize that she has followed these types of directions, dangerous directions, before.

"Do not look at anyone. Keep your face lowered so no one will ever remember you. When the train reaches Times Square, you will leave the train."

"Times Square?" Hana said, her voice brightening. "I have seen Times Square in the movies."

"Believe me, it is no film set. When you walk out of the subway, walk quickly uptown to 47th Street. There will be many people there. This is the difficult part."

"Difficult? Why?"

"It is harder to see if you are being followed when there is a crowd."

Hana took the hood of the sweatshirt and placed it over the top of her head. "No one knows I'm here."

"Well, someone does in Sarajevo. They sent you, remember? People see everyone. That's how I found him."

Sofia could taste the bile in her throat. Although it was only four days ago, the shock of seeing Stanislav still made her want to sink to her knees and vomit. She had been waiting at the bus stop on Broadway and 93rd Street. When the man with the cane stood beside her, she only acknowledged him as a blind old man. His overcoat was torn at the shoulders and his white thinning hair matted against his scalp. He stumbled as he entered the bus and Sofia caught a whiff of his unwashed odor. Yet, when she finally had a chance to look at him sitting in the front seat, she knew. The lightning bolt of a scar across his cheek was unique only to him, and although his eyes were hidden behind sunglasses, Stanislav's eyes would be that dark grey which was the same color as dirty ice. When he asked the bus conductor how many stops to Lincoln Center, his accent confirmed her suspicions. Decades had not changed that deep bass timbre that had called her, her mother and her grandmother filthy whores.

"You are absolutely sure?" Nick had asked her before he arranged for the gun.

"Yes,' Sofia had answered.

"Then I hope the bastard suffers when he dies," Nick said.

The monsters were everywhere, Sofia's mother told her. The Nazis who fled to America. One day you would hear on the news about the nice neighbor who fixed your car was really the Ukrainian concentration camp guard in charge of gassing a thousand prisoners a day. One of the most notorious Serbian war criminals, Radovan Karadzic, had been living for years as a holistic doctor in Belgrade, giving lectures and healing patients. No one suspected he was the force behind the notorious Srebrenica massacre. His patients, Sofia had read in a newspaper, "adored this kind and gentle man."

"Did he see you?" Hana asked, rubbing her lips as if to be sure all the lipstick was erased.

"No, he is blind, but he never looked at any of our faces, did he?"

Hana did not answer but Sofia knew she knew about Stanislav. Twenty-five years later the war had never truly ended for the older female members in their family. They were survivors of Vilina Vlas, now a spa in Bosnia, which once had been a rape and murder camp commandeered by Serbian nationalists. Several who survived would later commit suicide. Sofia's father and uncles did not speak of the war the same way as her mother and aunts. It is easier for the men to say the word genocide than whisper rape.

"When you get to 47th Street, walk four blocks to Eleventh Avenue." Sofia was now talking with her hands, as if pushing the air was in fact pushing Hana. "Walk quickly. Don't run, but move. Look for a red brick building with the number 544, 544 West 47th Street is his address. Ring the buzzer 4G. When you hear a voice, say that Al sent you."

Hana's brows furrowed as she frowned. "Al? Why?"

"Al is Stanislav's drug dealer and he'll ask you for a code word, which is Antonia, Stanislav's mother's name. What kind of sick bastard would use their mother's name for a drug code?"

"And then?"

"You know. This is why they paid you."

Suddenly the girl embraced Sofia. Her hair smelled like pine, like the old country. At first Sofia was stiff and then felt her limbs soften. Her eyelids swelled and she was scared she might weep.

"They trained me well," Hana said, her mouth brushing against her aunt's ear. "You are the brave one. I was too young, but I will never forget. Ajla, Vanessa, Zana."

"Nikoleta, Violeta," Sofia answered.

"Eminia, Lamija, Dalia." Hana's voice broke with the last name that belonged to her mother.

Sofia didn't remember if she embraced Hana before she left the laundry room. All she knew was that her knees buckled so she could barely stand. Sofia stumbled and collapsed into a plastic red chair. Closing her eyes, she envisioned Hana following her directions. Perhaps she will have trouble with the MetroCard and would have to swipe twice. Or the subway may be too crowded and she will have to wait for another train to pull into the station. Maybe Hana will be momentarily lost in Times Square, bewildered and astounded by the sheer volume of tourists. The bright neon billboards may mesmerize her, and although she has a mission, Hana could find herself gaping into a gaudily lit shop or a crowded theater lobby. As she walks toward Stanislav's apartment building, perhaps Hana bumps into two young teenage girls laughing; girls who do not have horrendous family pasts that follow them everywhere like a permanent cold night. These girls will be innocent forever. Hana will stop and stare at them, briefly imagining what it would be like to have grown up in America. When Stanislav opens the door, will she take out her gun, announce "Greetings from Sarajevo" and shoot him in the heart? Or will Hana just see a very old blind man, wearing a tattered bathrobe, a sad sickly invalid?

Hana was so very young. She was born after the war. Cities had healed. Young people could go to bars and concerts, flirt and love. They shouldn't have sent such a young girl, Sofia realized. They should have sent an older woman, a woman who remembered. A woman who hates.

A loud bell shrieked in the silence of the room. Sofia jumped and nearly knocked over the chair. It was only the finishing sound of the buzzer on the dryer. As she walked to the dryer she glanced at the clock: 8:30. In the corner was Hana's cheap black abandoned leather jacket. Sofia quickly snatched up the jacket and hid it beneath a pile of towels. The girl would need it when she returned.

THE LAST CAMP SOCIAL

"These are the facts of life," our camp bunk counselor Peggy would say, minutes before any camp social, glancing at her watch ticking away as if we were connected to the time bomb that each boy contained behind his jeans fly.

"The average teenage male's brain is soaked in sex," she told us, and I thought of a towel dropped in a bathtub, too heavy with water to wring.

As for the fourteen-year-old girls who were in her charge, we were no different than the boys. Maybe even more dangerous, our eggs all revved up and ready to go, like a souped-up Mustang in a drag race.

Peggy was from Arkansas—a state none of us had ever heard of and could have been as distant as Mars. Every morning she brushed her long bone-colored hair eighty strokes a minute and then massaged Vaseline into her scalp. She had lost her left eye to a stray golf ball, and in the empty pocket she could see miracles of light, bursts of purple, green and gold, a constellation of the Lord's color. A large gold crucifix flapped against her concave chest as Peggy shouted out directions for lifesaving as we swam in the cold Maine lake. She could teach us not to sink if our sailboats capsized but when it came to boys, we were all hell bent on drowning.

She prayed quietly in the middle of our cabin, her words competing with the buzzing mosquitoes and The Archie's "Sugar, Sugar." We traded lipsticks, practiced kissing our Bobby Sherman posters, tongues licking the crinkled paper that tasted like Cutter repellant. We, the girls of Cabin Nine, were all lost causes.

"Please stop," Peggy begged as we stuffed our bras with Kleenex.

Peggy also had the gift for predicting the future. One night, during a thunderstorm, she made us sit in a circle and announced our names: Cindy, Diana, Helen, Jill, Karen, Sylvia and Rachel. I wondered why I, Rachel, was the last on her list. Cindy, who wore thick-rimmed glasses and had braces, would be a film star. Diana, who was already a tennis star at the camp, would one day play at stadiums around the world. Helen would be a nurse, although we had seen Helen once faint at the sight of blood when she scraped her knee. Jill, the only girl who had divorced parents, would never be married but find happiness in a place filled with deserts and camels. Karen would have six children with three different men. As she spoke, her face would be lit up by the streaks of lightning outside. She never predicted anyone else's future because the electricity went out and we all screamed. "Now that's enough," she told us, leaving the cabin to inspect if there was damage outside our cabin because of the storm. Later that week I begged her to tell me what would happen to me, but she only took a deep breath and exhaled so deeply that I could feel her breath across my face.

That Sunday, the bus that took Peggy to church overturned and bounced down the mountain like a "yellow rubber ball," according to one witness. We did not know how to grieve, and just read our *Tiger Beat* magazines.

Our new counselor was named Summer, a beautiful California hippie who had been to Altamont and told us how she had seen the Hells Angels beat up people. Summer was the opposite of Peggy, and several of the girls sprayed lemon juice on their scalps so they could have her same butter blonde hair color.

Yet Peggy still hovered over us, her warnings hot against our skin like a sunburn that wouldn't heal. We couldn't explain to Summer why none of us wanted to attend that last camp social.

Instead, we sat in a circle outside our cabin, staring at the stars in the night sky, each girl holding each other's hands. This was our own memorial service. It was as if Peggy sacrificed herself for our collective virginity, our eggs safely nestled inside us mute and idle like dead car batteries.

THE ELEPHANT IN THE BUSH

"Look," my mother-in-law tells me. "There's an elephant in the bushes."

I turn to look where she is pointing. We are sitting on white deck chairs in a very suburban backyard in New Jersey.

"Do you see it?" She presses my hand. My mother-in-law, whose name is Ida, starts bobbing her head in the agitated way I now know so well.

"Of course," I tell her, taking off my sunglasses and peering at the shrubbery.

"How funny. Not only an elephant. But a baby elephant!"

Ida is in stage five of Alzheimer's disease. She is either a late five or early six. I've read the books her daughter has loaned me. *The 36-Hour Day* is the most popular book that is passed around from family member to family member.

I do not know if Ida knows my name. She does not remember that her son Gary left me ten years ago for a twenty-five-year-old nurse at his hospital. I have seen Ida more often than I have seen my ex-husband, who has moved to Anchorage, Alaska, and now has two sons with his second wife.

"Sister Teresa would never believe me if I had told her I saw a baby elephant. But then Sister Teresa was so nearsighted that she couldn't see much anyway," Ida says with a giggle.

Before Alzheimer's seized Ida's brain, she was very active in her town's synagogue and hosted Shabbat dinners every Friday. Sister Teresa is one of the nuns that hid Ida and her sister when they were children in Lodz, Poland. Luckily both sisters were blonde and the Nazi soldiers would come and bring the two little girls lollipops. The rest of Ida's family was sent to Auschwitz.

"Are you thirsty, Ida?" I ask. Phoebe, Ida's daughter, is picking up her little girl from a play date. She said she hoped I wouldn't mind watching her mother. Phoebe and her husband are doing their best to take care of Ida, but Ida frightens their daughter.

"Who are you?!" Ida once yelled at her eight-year-old granddaughter. "You're not my sister. Where is my sister?"

Ida's sister had died ten years ago in Philadelphia after being hit by a car in a supermarket parking lot. Mercifully Ida does not remember this.

"Are you thirsty?" I ask again. It's hot and it's important that she stays hydrated. Ida still does not answer my question. Her eyes glaze over like stale hard candy as she stares at her elephant in the bushes.

I visit Ida because I've always liked my mother-in-law. Ida made me laugh. She watched reruns of *I Love Lucy* and could do a very good imitation of Ethel. Halloween was her favorite holiday and one year she was a very convincing Dr. Ruth. At Passover, she would sink to her knees and crawl with the kids in search of the Afikomen. She never criticized Gary and me for choosing not to have kids. At this point, I doubt her new grandchildren in Alaska have even visited her.

"Sister Teresa was so beautiful," Ida continues. Today it seems we are stuck on the nuns in Poland. "Golden hair. Such blue eyes. She could have been a film star."

When the rabbi came to visit Ida, she refused to speak to him. "The house is not for sale," she told him.

"I don't want to buy your house, Mrs. Klein," the rabbi said.

"Then why are you here? Get out. I don't like the color of your shirt."

Ida started pacing up and down the hallway, repeating, "I don't like the color of your shirt" so many times that the poor rabbi had no choice but to leave. He has not returned.

I walk into the kitchen in order to get Ida a glass of water, all the time watching her from the back porch window. She isn't a runner, Ida. Not yet.

I bring her a glass of water and she stares. "I hope that's a gin and tonic."

I wonder where she is right now. I've never known Ida to drink a single drop of liquor.

"Of course it is," I tell her as I hand her the glass. She drains the water without a comment. A breeze blows through the backyard and I can smell the fumes of a nearby barbecue. A perfect June day, but who knows in what season Ida finds herself now.

"You're still here?" Ida asks. Is she talking to me or the elephant in the bush?

"Yes, I'm still here."

"Why?"

Why indeed? There was no reason why I had to stay connected to my ex-husband's family. I'm dating a nice man now, but I don't like visiting his mother who is an avid Republican and wears too much eyeliner. I like Ida, that's all. When Gary left me, I remember thinking that I wouldn't miss him but I would miss his mother. Now that she has Alzheimer's her daughter is so grateful that I am here to help.

The smoke from the barbecue rises in spirals above the roses by the fence. Ida sees them and stands up. Her face is ashen.

"Darling, what's wrong?" I ask. She is silent, staring at the fumes. Her hands are trembling. Memory can play so many dangerous games. Ida's face is rigid. Frozen. But she is still so beautiful. Her skin still so fine and smooth. This disease does not ravage your face.

Then I see it. The bees by the bush.

"The elephant," Ida murmurs. "They'll sting the baby elephant."

Heroically, insanely, I run toward the bees. Let them just try to sting me. Miraculously, they buzz away. I return to Ida and her trembling hands are now applauding.

"Well done, Susan!"

She knows me. She knows my name.

When I turn around once more to look at the bush, I realize: One branch is a trunk. Another branch is the head. A third branch the body. In a certain slant of light, it's possible. I can see the elephant too.

DOCTOR WALES

I was in eighth grade and in big trouble. That was why I was sent to see Dr. Wales.

When I entered the doctor's office, his book, *How To Save Your Starving Daughter* was featured on all of the shelves. The cover was a shadow of a skeletal girl, with Dr. Wales' smiling bearded face and reassuring mop of hair floating beneath the frightening illustration. On a round table was a small gold square plaque with OUTSTANDING BOOK FOR PARENTS engraved in large block letters. It looked rather like a shrine to me, and I fought the urge to kneel down. I was, after all, meeting the rock star of shrinks for teenage girls.

My mother told me she had to pull "serious strings" to achieve this appointment with the famous Dr. Roger Wales. Various photographs of Dr. Wales with talk show hosts like Phil Donahue were prominently displayed in the office. In every photograph he clutched his book against his chest like a security blanket. Roger Wales sounded to me more like a name of an actor than a psychologist.

When his office door finally opened and a voice beckoned me inside, I saw that Dr. Wales had cut his hair and shaved his beard. He looked younger, and his eyes were a much more vivid blue than the photographs in the waiting room. He wore corduroy pants, the same pin-striped dressed shirt that all my male teachers wore, with a nutty brown tweed jacket with leather patches on the elbows. I noticed that his hands were small, almost as if someone had transplanted children's hands onto an adult body.

"Welcome Kate," he told me. "Grab a chair." His voice was thrilling: deep and hearty, the kind of voice that Santa uses in cartoons.

I looked around his office. There were at least five chairs, including a bean bag. I sat in the chair nearest the door, a hardback chair that made me sit straight. On the wall were framed posters of rock bands that were popular in the 1970s: The Eagles, Boston and

The Cars. I guessed that the posters were supposed to make his patients feel like they were in their own bedroom.

"I didn't do it," I told the doctor, trying not to cry as my eyes brimmed with tears. I noticed the Kleenex box on his desk. No, I wouldn't stoop to use it.

"Can you explain to me what happened?" Dr. Wales said, stroking his chin as if looking for a lost beard.

What happened was that my mother had found three nickel bags of marijuana hidden beneath my bras in my closet. The marijuana was stored in zip lock bags. The kind of bag she used to make me tuna fish belonged to my friend Gina, whose father had happened to be a federal judge. She was terrified that her own father would send her to jail, and anyway, the marijuana didn't belong to her but to Ralph, her college freshman boyfriend at NYU who asked Gina to save it for him during Thanksgiving break since he didn't trust his roommate. Gina asked me if I could hide it for her and that Ralph would pick it up that Monday after Thanksgiving. The problem was that Ralph was involved in a motorcycle accident near New Paltz and would not be at NYU for the rest of the semester. That meant I had to hold on to the marijuana—until the housekeeper found it and promptly delivered the three bags to my mother.

I didn't think my mother would even know what marijuana looked like—she was so removed from my teenage world that she thought Pink Floyd might be the name of a shade of paint. I was wrong. She had watched some terrible afterschool special about a cheerleader on her way to Harvard and the next day dead with a needle in her arm—with marijuana the gateway drug. It was terrible to watch her sob; tears leaking from her fingers as she covered her face with her hands. My father was in Tokyo involved in a deal. If he wasn't in Tokyo he was somewhere else like Kuwait or Rio. I never truly understood what my father did, and my mother just said that he pushed a lot of money around in the world.

I told Dr. Wales the truth. He nodded slowly, and rubbed his small hands together.

"And your mother didn't believe you?" he asked.

"No. She said I was a drug addict and that if I didn't see you I would die."

"Well you're not going to die. She must be pleased you don't have an eating disorder."

I looked down at my thighs which weren't exactly slender and didn't know if I should take that as a compliment or as something else.

"I'm fine," I told Dr. Wales. "I shouldn't even be here."

"Well now that you're here, there is a topic that I bring up with my young female patients. Shockingly, a topic for which they express complete ignorance."

I leaned in as Dr. Wales grabbed a white piece of paper from his typewriter, took out a ballpoint pen from his jacket pocket and began to draw frantically. After a few moments he looked up at me, his blues eyes even brighter.

"Do you know what a clitoris is, Kate?"

A clitoris. It was a word maybe I heard in our mandatory sex education class. I remember my friend Jill saying it sounded like a contagious disease.

"Just what I expected," the doctor told me, giving me the piece of paper. "Here look at this."

I examined his drawing. What I saw resembled a peanut shell caught in a V.

"The time will come when you will need to educate your male partner about this part of your body. Boys are terribly ignorant. To know your body is to know power."

My cheeks were beginning to burn. Why was he telling me this? I thought I was here because of drugs. Dr. Wales' face was flushed as well. The white page from the typewriter that he gave me with the diagram felt damp. I quickly placed it in my bag next to my pencil case and Spearmint chewing gum.

"Do you have a boyfriend?"

I shook my head. I was madly in love with Josh Wilson, the Ultimate Frisbee champion in our high school, but so were about fifteen other girls in my class.

"Well then, I wouldn't worry. To be honest, I sense that you have low self-esteem."

My head jerked up in surprise. Dr. Wales was still staring so intently at me that I tried to move three inches away but the hard chair seat prevented me.

"I'm fine," I mumbled.

"Don't worry. You'll grown into your looks. You're just in what we call an awkward phase."

Awkward phase. I know I wasn't thin and my hair was frizzy and my nose a bit big but still…

"Do you think I'm ugly?" I asked, my voice quivering.

"No, no. I didn't mean that. When you look in the mirror, how would you rate yourself?"

"From one to ten?"

'Yes. From one to ten."

"A five?" I said, knowing he would correct me, that I was surely at least a seven.

Doctor Wales' eyes traveled from the top of my head to the pennies in my loafers. "Yes, at this moment, I suppose that's accurate."

He continued chatting about the importance of not succumbing to society's expectations of beauty, to ignore the covers of *Seventeen* magazine and how playing a sport would make me feel more confident about my body. I wasn't listening to him anymore. I kept thinking he didn't say I was higher than a five.

The session was soon over. A very skinny teenage girl wearing a fake pink fur jacket was slumped in a chair in the waiting room, gnawing at a nail. I wondered what number rating Dr. Wales would assign to her. I took out his drawing of a clitoris and crumpled it up and threw it in the white wastebasket by the door. The girl looked up at me from her heavily purpled shaded lids. I waited until she was ushered into the office until I achieved what I really wanted. The gold award for his book shone in the bright light. I grabbed it, placed it in my bag and raced down the hallway, pushing the elevator button frantically. In the subway station, I dumped it into a trash bin where it fell with a satisfying thud. It felt good to see his award there with crumpled copies of *The New York Post* and empty Coke cans.

For days I was terrified that Dr. Wales would call my mother. But he never did. When she asked me what I thought of him I told her he said I didn't need to see him anymore and I would never ever smoke marijuana, which was true, since just once joint gave me a blinding headache. I was too embarrassed to confide in her about his diagram or his opinion of my attractiveness. But my mother wasn't paying much attention to me. My father had just confessed to her about his infidelity with a dental hygienist and was begging her forgiveness.

Several years later I saw Dr. Wales on a syndicated talk show. He had moved on from adolescence girls to middle-aged woman. His new book was titled *How To Find The New You In You*. I wondered now with my hair straightened and my skin clear if he would still rate me as a five. But I didn't care. I was in love with my college boyfriend who said I was beautiful.

"How would you rate me?" I asked. "You know, in looks."

Once again, I felt the shame and anger I felt as Dr. Wales rated me a five.

"12," my boyfriend answered. "Hey gorgeous, come back to bed."

I had already found and understood by clitoris by now. My boyfriend pushed away the sheets as I nestled next to him. 12. Go to hell, Dr. Wales, I thought as my boyfriend kissed me again and again.

WEST END GIRL

Summer of 1977 was when I first fell in love. That was also the summer of Son of Sam., the killer who was terrorizing New York City. Lurid headlines blazed from the front page of newspapers and all my friends in tenth grade were cutting their hair because the Son of Sam supposedly liked girls with long hair. I kept my hair pinned up in a bun. He hadn't shot anyone with that hairstyle yet. Disco music, like a noxious fume, was everywhere. I hated that pulsating rhythm and incessant beat. Donna Summer moaned with one orgasm after another.

In the basement of the Ansonia apartment building, where my piano teacher lived, was a notorious swingers club called Plato's Retreat. Supposedly, naked people lined up for a lavish buffet and then had orgies in a heavily chlorinated pool. One rule was that single men were not allowed to enter the club. Sometimes a lone man would approach me on my way to my piano lesson at night, offering me fifty dollars just to walk in with them through the front door.

"Don't worry," they told me. "You don't have to go inside." I wouldn't touch their dollars that looked as limp as soggy leaves. Those men resembled my dentist, fat and pasty with Long Island accents.

At sixteen, I had very limited experience with boys. There had been awkward kissing and groping in eighth-grade games of Spin the Bottle, and a boy at a party who grabbed my breast as if he were testing a grapefruit. When I slapped him hard, he actually began to cry. I attended an all-girl camp with very strict counselors. We were checked daily to be sure we were wearing bras in case one of the boys from our brother camp wandered into our territory. Unlike my cousin Maureen, who had been sleeping with boys since eighth grade and was already on the pill, I felt woefully ignorant. "Just wait," Maureen told me. I didn't want just sex. I wanted to be possessed, the same way as my favorite literary lovers, Cathy and

Heathcliff. But, as Maureen reminded me, their affair did not end well.

The man I fell in love with worked at a bar by Columbia University called The West End.

How did a sixteen-year-old girl hang out in a bar? In 1977 no one paid much attention to rules. There were more important things to worry about with a madman terrorizing the city. I was tall, looked older, and the drinking age was 18, only two years away. The bar was dark even in the summer day, as if light was an unwelcome customer. How I hated the sun! I avoided the beach no matter how many times my parents pleaded with me to join them at The Jersey Shore. I was so pale that teenage boys cruising in cars would lean out of their window and yell, "Hey Casper, get a tan!" The city sun was merciless. The glare from the concrete sidewalk could blind you, and the stifling heat felt like a clammy dance partner that clung to you with a sweaty embrace. The Lovin' Spoonful had it wrong. There was nothing enticing about "summer in the city."

You could usually find at The West End at least three college freshmen clutching worn copies of *On the Road*, as well as a professor reeking of bourbon who would talk all night about how he spent a crazy weekend with Neal Cassidy at Allen Ginsberg's Greenwich Village studio. Victor was one of the bartenders. He was tall and dark and skinny. There are no skinny men anymore since the boom of the gym culture, and I miss that sinuous and slender sexiness of men. Victor's face was all cheekbones, and he would have been almost pretty if not for his nose that looked slightly broken. His black eyes were as shiny as beads and he had longer lashes than mine. At night I would imagine those lashes fluttering over my hot skin like tiny brushes.

I liked to watch him when he wasn't mixing drinks, standing at the end of the bar, drumming his fingers on a napkin to an invisible jazz beat. I would sit unsteadily on a wobbly stool and wish I were wearing a brilliant piece of jewelry that would shine in the darkness so he could see me. Some nights no one else sat at the bar, and the space around me seemed to swirl about in pockets of cool air. If only he would notice me, I prayed over and over. One night, he did.

I was bending down to fix a broken strap of my sandal. When I looked up, Victor was standing right in front of me, his face only inches away from mine. His olive skin looked slicked and moist as if he had just stepped out of the shower.

"What do you want?" he asked, and then, perhaps because I didn't answer fast enough, he repeated the question. "What do you want?" His voice had surprised me. He didn't sound confident but actually unsure, as if he were the customer who couldn't decide what to order.

I ordered a Coke because I was terrified he would ask for my ID. I watched him fill the glass with three square ice cubes and then pour liquid the color of molasses from a bottle. When Victor returned and gave me my drink I could feel the warmth of his fingerprints on the cool glass. I didn't dare look up into his face but stared down into the bubbles. Finally, when I glanced again, I saw that Victor had retreated to his favorite end of the bar where he stared at a red neon exit sign and resumed drumming his fingers on the napkin.

I drank the Coke too quickly, the sweetness making me feel queasy in a way, as if I had just eaten too much candy. I kept gulping the soda until the ice cubes rattled against my teeth. All I could see was Victor's back, his shirt the same red as that neon sign. All that redness seemed to burn right through my eyes and into the back of my head. I felt as if Victor turned around to look at me I would melt like the ice cube in my now warm soda. Never before had I craved so intensely for someone to touch me. The air conditioner blew across my shoulder and my skin prickled with goose bumps.

One of the musicians from the jazz room walked into the bar and shouted, "My man, Victor!" and I saw my bartender nod. "Victor," I whispered to myself, his name as cool and smooth as the glass in my palm.

West End Girl

I had plenty of time to kill at The West End. The summer camp, which had hired me as a counselor, had to fire everyone since there seemed to be no children who wanted to enroll. My friends were either in Europe or at their parents' summer homes in Long Island. Manhattan, in July, seemed to be an abandoned waste site, either because of the heat or Son of Sam.

"You're not bored, are you?" my mother asked, and I lied and said I was hanging out at The New York Public Library reading my high school summer books. I never came home because there were four days of the week when Victor had the day shift, which started at noon and ended by eight. I preferred the bar during the day. No drunk fraternity boys to bother me, and the late afternoon drinkers were mostly middle-aged working-class men, taxi drivers or doormen on their breaks who were more interested in their scotch than conversation. I was probably the one person in the bar who was not drinking liquor. But I didn't need alcohol to feel intoxicated. Just glancing once into Victor's black liquid eyes was enough. Sometimes when his fingers brushed against mine, I would suddenly pull away, as if I had just touched fire. Now I wonder if anyone noticed me at all; a teenage girl who, hour after hour, nursed a watery Coke, my eyes always focused on the bartender moving as gracefully as a ballet dancer on his stage.

I noticed small things about him daily: how his nails were cut shorter than usual, or that his hair was parted on the left instead of the right, or one Friday, he wore a necklace with a thick gold cross. His lips always looked to me as if he had just licked them. At night, alone in my bed, I would wonder how his mouth would taste on my lips, how they would feel on my body.

"Go home sweetheart, this is a place of stale beer and staler men," the alcoholic professor told me one night when I stood up from my stool at 8 PM, which was the end of Victor's shift. I never followed him outside the bar onto Broadway. I didn't want to see him outside the bar. It was as if there, on the steaming sidewalk on the Upper West Side, Victor could just dissolve.

Although we never had a conversation, I could eavesdrop through the din of loud talk and music and learn about Victor. Bartending wasn't his true calling, but jazz. He much preferred hanging out at the jazz room than being trapped behind an army of glasses. No matter who was waiting for a drink, Victor always gave the musicians a free round. He loved Charlie Parker and Miles Davis and Billie Holiday. He would hum a tune I soon learned was "Strange Fruit." At precisely six, the chef from the kitchen would deliver Victor a bowl of chili and a baked potato. That was the only meal Victor would eat. I noticed that he never drank alcohol, even though many of his patrons offered to buy him a round. Victor only drank tea with two slices of lemon, holding the cup daintily as he took small tentative sips from the steaming liquid.

I was not his only admirer. These were not girls or even ladies, but real women. There was a large black woman named Louise Johnson who sang jazz in the back room and always wore low-cut sequined dresses to reveal her ample bosom. "Hey Victor sweetheart," she would croon. "When are you going to join my jam session?"

A waitress with a Debbie Harry bleached blonde haircut and purple lipstick would place her pale hands with black polished nails on his wrist and whisper in his ear. One night a beautiful Asian woman wearing a sleeveless blue silk sheath walked up to the bar, whispered his name, and when he appeared, leaned over to kiss his lips for what seemed like a full minute. I was there forever in every second of that kiss. When Victor finally broke for air, I was astounded that there was no impression of her shiny red lipstick on his mouth.

Then there was the angry woman. Perhaps she was once beautiful, but her fury seemed to make her black hair stand on its end, and her white face was bleached with misery. "Damn you to hell, Victor," she shouted, throwing a set of keys into his face. Victor ducked, and the clanking keys fell into a pitcher of beer. It would have almost been funny had the woman not started weeping. Victor quickly walked from behind the bar and with a hand on the woman's shoulder, swiftly lead her to the back of the room. I saw him speak urgently to her while her head bobbed up and down, still crying. When she finally exited, a violent streak of white light pierced the darkness and made me wince. "Go home," the old professor whispered to me touching me briefly with a hand as brown and weathered as leather. "Now."

But I didn't want to be at home, listening to news reports about the lunatic terrorizing New York City. I wanted to be that sobbing woman who at least had held Victor in her arms. I wanted to feel the fire, the sizzle, a heat that boiled across my breasts and sizzled toward my belly. That summer of 1977 was hot, but not hot enough.

Then one day it happened. It had been perhaps three weeks since I had been sitting on my stool, sipping Coke after Coke, watching Victor for hours. I went to the restroom in the dingy back hall and when I pushed open the door, I felt a smooth hand grasp my wrist.

"What do you want?" Victor asked me, pulling me closer toward him. "What do you want?"

His arms were surprisingly strong for such a slender man, and I felt so fragile smashed up against him. Even if I wanted to answer him, I couldn't. He kissed me hard, and when I opened my mouth, he tasted of lemons. His lips were softer than I expected, and I could hear myself make a deep sound. Above my head the red neon exit sign burned in my eyes. Although Victor must have kissed me for only a minute, it seemed like an eternity, a black hole where I was falling, falling, thrilled at the speed of the descent. Just as suddenly as he took me, he abruptly let go, his arms raised as if just arrested.

"Is that what you want?" he asked me. He was frowning and his voice sounded confused. "Is that what you really want?"

Someone called out, "Hey Victor, we need you in the kitchen," and Victor headed to the back. The air-conditioning was making me shiver and I suddenly craved the warmth outside. I managed to make my way to the front door and opened it. The harsh sunlight startled me and I had to squint against the glare. Crossing Broadway I bumped into a woman who cursed me. I didn't see her.

I barely heard her. When our bodies collided, I couldn't feel her. Victor's kiss still stung on my lips yet the rest of me was insensate.

That night my parents told me we were leaving for Cape Cod the next morning. They were worried about my restlessness, my lack of direction. Someone in our apartment building, my parents wouldn't tell me who, had seen me at The West End. Although my mother didn't ask any questions, she knew that I was in trouble. And I was in trouble. I knew that if I returned to The West End, I would want to see Victor again and do more than just see him. I wanted him to take me into the darkness where there was jazz and magic and heat. I didn't know if he would agree but I would make him.

I went to Hyannis with my family and there wasn't a minute during our vacation when I wasn't seeing, hearing, feeling or breathing Victor. At night, I tried to duplicate his touch but failed. At every restaurant in Cape Code I asked for lemon slices, hoping to reproduce his tart taste in my mouth. The bartenders were mostly tanned college boys in bright Lacoste shirts the colors of ice cream, too clean and fresh for me. These polished wooden counters reminded me of a new bowling alley. The floors were so clean that I expected them to squeak. How I longed for the sawdust-strewn floor of The West End Bar, littered with discarded half-smoked cigarettes and sometimes broken glass.

We returned just in time for my last year of high school. I was busy with new classes, new teachers, and catching up with friends. That August, David Berkowitz was arrested and his reign of murderous terror was finally over. The city seemed to sigh in relief and all the girls in my class let their hair grow long again. The West End didn't seem real to me anymore, more like a film I saw one hot summer night. When I thought about Victor, I wasn't even sure about his age. Teenage girls were not supposed to be with adult men. There was a new boy in my class named Adam who kissed me in a taxi. Yet his mouth missed mine and our teeth clinked. I knew I had to return to The West End.

But Victor was gone. I knew it the moment I saw the new young bartender with a gold earring who stood in Victor's place, slowly pouring golden amber beer from a green bottle into a glass. The old professor who had told me to go home sat hunched at a back table, coils of cigarette smoke floating above his head. I would return a week later, a month later, even a year later, but Victor never returned. The black bartender was replaced by a young Hispanic woman who would be replaced by another bartender, a young white man with a wisp of a red moustache and angry red eyes. Nothing felt the same. The bar stool where I once sat was now a high wooden chair, the Coke tasted flat, and there were new bright lights that only served to illuminate the ashes on the counter, the dust motes in the air. Not only was Victor gone, but so was The West End.

Now, in 2022, The West End Bar has truly vanished. The owners had sold it to a Cuban restaurant that went out of business way before the pandemic. I am probably now the same age as the bearded Columbia University professor who spoke devoutly of Ginsberg and Kerouac.

I stand in front of the boarded windows and the shuttered doors. Young and old walk swiftly past me as the sky begins to darken and rain begins to fall. I think of the famous line from The Great Gatsby: "*So we beat on, boats against the current, borne back ceaselessly into the past.*" I never really understood that quote until now. The years are like an endless stream, pulling you back no matter how hard you resist. The past should be gone. Yet as I listen closely, I can still hear strains of jazz music, like a hidden fragrance escaping an empty bottle. I can still taste the cold Coke soda fizzing in my mouth, feel my hands gripping the wooden bar as I wait for Victor to appear. I am sixteen again, filled with the sadness and madness of that youthful love. No one could kiss me the way Victor had kissed me, because Victor had been the first.

"What do you want?" he had asked me so many decades ago.

I should have replied, "Just you."

ECHO BEACH

I.

Resting at the southernmost point of Montego Bay, Jamaica, stood Echo Beach Hotel.

I was eleven years old and sitting on the beach in the shade of a large umbrella with Juliet.

"Gollywogs," cried Juliet.

"What's that?" I asked.

"They're all over. The people who work here. Can't you see?"

I was from New York. Juliet, also eleven, was from England. Her mother made Juliet wear a thick mask of Coppertone, a white beach robe and a white floppy hat. She looked like a funny ghost.

"Darling," Juliet's mother cried in her screechy English accent from her beach chair. Even from this distance, I could smell her coconut suntan oil. "Please leave those poor crabs alone."

Juliet's favorite activity was gathering hermit crabs from the sea and pulling their twitching bodies out of their shells. I thought this was terrible, but still watched with fascination. At night I had nightmares of Juliet drowning in a sea of pale mutilated shells.

This was the first time Juliet's family had come to Jamaica, but my fourth. My parents spent their honeymoon there and Echo Beach was their "special" place, always spoken in revered tones.

"Gollywogs," Juliet said again. "I have dolls at home."

I had no idea what Juliet was talking about and wanted to leave. My parents kept pushing me to play with her since they spent most of the time at The Cypress Bar and slept till noon. To get away from Juliet, I told her I wanted to go swimming. Juliet didn't know how to swim and sulked back to the hotel.

I walked away to the far side of the beach. The sand burned. The sunlight looked orange, but everything looked orange in Jamaica. As I waded through the water, I was mesmerized by the shells and swirling grains of sand, the water lapping at my ankles, until I looked up and I realized I was lost. This part of the beach was empty. Several amber-colored beer bottles littered the sand and a torn pink umbrella was positioned upside down. The sand felt grittier. I knew I wasn't too far from the hotel because I could still hear the calypso music the band played every noon. Someone was singing my favorite song:

"Good morning, Mr. Walker

I've come to see your daughter.

Sweet Rosemary...

Tell me she's going to marry me."

A tall man was walking on the beach. He wore a white t-shirt and sunglasses and his hands were thrust in the pockets of his khaki pants. I didn't recognize him at first, but the man was Trevor, the chief bartender at The Cypress Bar at the hotel. My parents spent hours there. I was constantly sulking because I disliked being stuck on a stool with a Coke. But Trevor always had kind words for me. He had been born in London but moved to Jamaica when he was my age. Trevor would tell me he never could get rid of his British accent and all the children at school would laugh at him, calling him "Limey." His accent was different than Juliet's and her mother's, more precise yet warmer.

"My dear Claire," Trevor said. "Whatever are you doing here?"

"Hello Trevor," I answered.

"Well, this is a coincidence. I was hoping to see you. I've just found something for you. And just for you and no one else."

Trevor took his hand out of his pocket and revealed the most beautiful shells I had ever seen. They were so tiny and white that they reminded me of pearls. He brought his closed fist to my hand and deposited the shells in my palm.

"They're beautiful," I told him. I wanted to keep them forever. But I was scared I would lose them.

"Will you keep them for me?" I asked Trevor.

"But this is a present for you."

"Please?"

Trevor sensed my distress because he opened his hand and I gently pored the shells into his open palm.

"Why aren't you on the beach?" he asked.

"But this is the beach," I answered.

"No dear. Hotel guests are not supposed to be here. Did you not read the sign?"

I vaguely remembered seeing bright red letters but had not paid any attention. At the end of the beach was a gate of twisted barbed wire. Beyond that gate I could make out a road with several figures walking slowly in the sun.

"Juliet's horrible!" I suddenly exclaimed.

"And why's that?"

"She likes to kill crabs. Trevor, what are Gollywogs?"

"Did Juliet say that word?"

"Yes. That's what she called the people who work here."

I realized too late that Trevor would be connected too with that name.

Trevor whistled and his eyes narrowed. "My, isn't she a very English little girl."

"But what does that mean?" I asked.

Trevor paused for a moment and then shook his head. He told me to turn around and return to the hotel beach. He had to report to the dining room, change into his uniform and set up that afternoon's tea. I asked Trevor if I could help but he answered that my mother and father wouldn't like that at all, so I hid in the shadows of a palm tree, watching him walk swiftly across the sand. He even moved differently than the other Jamaicans, his back held straight, his stride determined. Trevor's fingers were always snapping to an invisible beat I imagined was to the tune of my song, "Good Morning, Mr. Walker."

I did not know where to go or what to do. I didn't want to see my parents; they were always cranky after they woke up from their afternoon nap and would stay in bed drinking rum and ice until it was time for cocktail hour. The sunburn on my forehead was hurting.

I decided to play with the umbrella I had seen earlier and started dragging it to the edge of the beach near the sidewalk. The umbrella was heavy and I was hot, but I was determined to bring that umbrella to the gate. With tremendous effort I picked it up and laid it straight against the barbed wire. Now that gate did not look so ugly anymore. I stood there, admiring my work, when I became aware of another viewer. A little black boy stood only a few inches away from me, wearing only white underpants. His limbs were covered in a thin layer of sand that looked like sugar and almost his whole fist was jammed in his mouth. The little boy walked up to what I thought of as my umbrella and began pulling at it. Incensed that he was taking it, I grabbed the umbrella and hauled it back up again.

"Be careful!" I told the boy in a loud voice. "You don't want to hurt yourself."

He stood still for a moment, then seized the umbrella and started tugging at it again. A possessive fury overcame me. How dare this boy take my umbrella? I was surprised by how easy it was to lift him. With a strength that surprised me, I swung him over my left side and watched, stunned, as he fell noiselessly into the sand. I was terrified that he was hurt—that he would start howling, that I would get into trouble. But the boy remained motionless and then began babbling in a quiet even voice. He did not sound upset, though at some points he would raise his voice as if I had said something wrong. I had no idea what to do. Before I knew it, he was running. As I watched him take off, I saw in my mind how my day would unfold, boring hours ahead of watching Juliet torture those poor crabs, her mother yelling at her, me feeling listless and trapped. I didn't want another empty day like that, so I decided to follow him.

Beyond the gate, the road was filled with dust and empty beer bottles. A donkey stood munching dry grass. The boy ran very fast and I could not keep up with him. A skinny goat trotted along, staring at me with yellow eyes. There were no cars on the road, and to the left was a large heap of broken bicycles without tires. The boy seemed to be heading toward a cluster of huts painted red and white. There were no windows. The porches were covered with dirty plates, chicken bones and empty cans. The boy stopped suddenly and put his fist in his mouth again. A very old woman with white hair came out on the porch and stared at me with bloodshot eyes. For a few moments she did not speak, but only clucked her tongue.

"You turn around," she finally said. "You turn around and go back. Understand?"

I couldn't move. The woman repeated this and then several people came out of their huts. There were three men, all bare-chested, wearing rainbow-striped knitted caps that did not completely hide their glossy coils of hair. The woman slapped the boy so hard across the face that my hand flew up to my mouth in horror. The boy looked stunned and then burst into tears. Another old lady watched me as she strung blue beads with a large needle. She opened a little cloth bag at her side and a whole strand of bright blue beads spilled out across the porch and onto the road. The blue beads were so big that I thought they looked like eyeballs, staring at me accusingly. I stumbled back to the beach, my thoughts a blur, not wanting to think about that poor boy. I imagined those beads watching me all the way back to my hotel rom.

II.

Four years later I told Trevor about this incident. He was making a large pitcher of Pina Coladas for that evening's cocktail party and listened to me intently. I still couldn't shake the image of that day. I felt I had transgressed in some way, but I couldn't say how. The boy had invited me to run after him, but I knew I wasn't supposed to follow. Everyone thought this was for my safety, yet he was the one who ended up hurt. Not only by the woman who slapped him, but also by me, for I had picked him up and tossed him—though I didn't share this part with Trevor.

"It was wrong of you to follow that little boy back to his home," Trevor told me. "What would you have told your parents? They would have said something to the manager, who would have found out whose little boy he was, and then made trouble with the police."

I sulked in my seat. I was fifteen and believed everyone was against me.

"Here, Claire. You can have just one sip but don't tell anyone."

Trevor sometimes allowed me to sample his concoctions without the liquor added. Even though I knew there wasn't alcohol in these cocktails I still felt dizzy, as if I drank three Coconut Crèmes in a row.

"I live there too," Trevor said softly. For a moment, I didn't know what he was talking about. Then I realized that his home must also be located amongst those huts. Somehow, I had believed that Trevor lived in the hotel—maybe even in a room similar to my own. He seemed so intimately connected with Echo Beach

"It's a beautiful day, Claire," Trevor told me. "Go outside and swim. This is no place to spend your vacation."

"My parents are driving me crazy," I moaned. "I wish I had stayed home."

"You're just angry. Everyone is angry at your age." Trevor leaned over and smelled like the limes he had been slicing. "Shall we have a cup of tea?"

I felt a warm rush of feeling through me. Our teatime together was my secret, my special place at Echo Beach. I followed Trevor into the back kitchen. There was always a teakettle on the burner. He was very strict about making tea—the water had to be ice cold before it boiled, and the tea bags needed to steep at least five minutes. I loved the smell of hot water and soapy suds, the soothing ritual of making British tea.

"England ruined me," he once told me. "Here, I'm not Jamaican. There, I was never British."

I knew Trevor felt deeply betrayed by the country that refused to accept him. His family was invited to England after the war as guest workers, but forced to leave after their shop was burned down.

"Please sing 'Jerusalem' to me again," I asked Trevor then. This was, according to Trevor, England's official anthem, a song he proudly told me he had once sang when the Queen's cousin came to visit his school.

"Not today, love," Trevor said. He lit a cigarette and I watched a silver wreath of smoke float up to the ceiling and disappear. He passed me a tray of Edinburgh shortbread biscuits and we both nibbled in comforting silence. Our shared solace seemed as golden as the sun, which shone through the window and illuminated the crystal glasses in the serving trays. Someone outside called out his name.

"Do you have to leave?" I asked him.

"I wish I could spend more time, but work is work," Trevor said, standing up and grabbing a dishrag for the bar.

Outside Juliet was perched on a bar stool, water dripping from her wet hair. "Hullo Claire. Hullo there, Trevor. Claire, why aren't you on the beach? It's brilliant outside."

Guests were not supposed to wear bathing suits inside the hotel, but Juliet went everywhere in her green string bikini. Her mother had died and her father's new wife was only twenty-five. The two shared clothes and cosmetics.

Over the past couple of years, Juliet and I had written letters, at first one or two a year, but then picking up pace. Our letters couldn't get to each other across the ocean fast enough. I had forgotten I had disliked her once. She was now funny and charming. We traded secrets. Whenever we saw each other again at Echo Beach, we were able to resume our friendship as if we had never left the hotel.

"Claire refuses to leave me," Trevor told her with a wink.

"Who can blame her?" Juliet asked with a grin. She was always flirting with Trevor and the rest of the hotel staff.

I thought back to when Juliet had compared crabs to Golliwogs. Last year, I had looked them up, seen the racist images of black rag dolls in England, comic and minstrel. I thought about how Juliet had seen the bulging eyes in the faces of the crabs, thought about how she had mutilated their bodies.

"Come on, Claire," Juliet whined. "Sit with me on the beach."

I was furious with Juliet's intrusion, but I knew I couldn't spend all day with Trevor in the bar. We said good-bye to him and walked out into the glaring sunlight.

"There's a party," Juliet told me. "At The Lucky Irene. Let's go."

There was always a party on the boat called The Lucky Irene. It was a yacht that never seemed to sail anywhere. The owner was the widow of the hotel's original owner. She had her own special table in the middle of the dining room, which she shared with a series of Jamaican men. The man who was now with Irene was tall and elegant and always wore white suits with a slender shimmering gold watch. Irene was a woman in her sixties with jowls like a bulldog and eyebrows haphazardly painted on. Her loud laugh was metallic and cold and could be heard from her yacht at night.

Juliet told me to meet her in thirty minutes in the lobby and to look sharp. I only had a black dress with spaghetti straps made of some nylon material that made my skin itch. Juliet wore a glittery gold dress and gold sandals with tottering high heels. Her eye shadow sparkled, and the perfume she wore smelled like her late mother's cocoa butter oil.

The deck of The Lucky Irene had been transformed into a ballroom. Chandeliers of candles seemed to hang from the night sky. A steel band played calypso. Pretty Jamaican women served rum in carved-out pineapples. Juliet and I hid in a corner and watched the shadows of the guests glide across the water.

Irene wore a ruby red dress with a long shimmering scarf that trailed behind her back. Her Jamaican was stunning in his white suit and carried a bottle of champagne. No one spoke to him except Irene who kept whispering in his ear. One torchlight seemed to attach itself to his gold watch and it made my eyes hurt when I looked. The drummer of the calypso band began pounding on his drums. They brought a limbo stick out on the deck and torched it with a high flame.

"Show time," Irene cried out. "My friends, may I introduce you to The Wonderful Wanda."

Wanda was a Jamaican girl, only a few years older than me. The plastic fruit precariously perched on her head seemed always on the verge of sliding off. Her Hawaiian grass skirt was too big for her and had to be held together at the waist with a large safety pin. She looked awkward and uncomfortable—too young for her clothes, too earnest. When she thought no one was looking, she even gnawed at a fingernail. What was she doing here? But still everyone applauded as Wanda smiled nervously and bobbed her head.

The torchlight reflected in her eyes, making them glow. The girl placed her hands on her hips and leaned all the way back until her head touched the floor. Then, to the rhythm of the conga, she shimmied beneath the fiery stick and slowly stood up with raised palms. The act was repeated over and over again, each time with an increasingly louder drumbeat. A troupe of men singing "Yellowbird" joined her. Several drunken guests tried to dance beneath the limbo stick themselves, and a fat man became stuck and the crowd roared with laughter.

"Yellowbird," Irene sang, her voice screeching above the musicians. Her Jamaican suddenly left her side and strode out onto the dance floor. He lifted the limbo stick so the fat man could stand up, and walked over to Wanda.

Gently taking her by the arm, he said "enough." His voice was calm yet seemed as loud as the Congo drums. He swept his hand in a small circle, indicating the yacht, the musicians, and the torches. "I am leaving," he told Irene. "I do not want to do this anymore."

Irene stared at him with an open mouth as he took off his white jacket and draped it over Wanda's trembling shoulders. "Go home," he calmly said to her. "You'll still get your money." The calypso players stopped singing and stared sheepishly at each other, unsure what to do next. There were whisperings among the guests. It was very quiet on the deck of The Lucky Irene as the people moved silently toward the bar.

At first I wanted to tell Trevor about the party, then decided not to let him know I had been there. I also felt upset about the man in the white suit's rebellion. I knew he had been right, but hotel guests paid a lot of money to get the Jamaica they wanted. Echo Beach seemed suddenly different to me. It was like finding a beautiful shell on the beach and turning it over, discovering it covered with maggots. But I wasn't one of the white tourists in that boat who had watched her. Why hadn't I said or done anything? I felt dirty and even nauseated. The girl had looked so scared.

I tried to talk to Juliet about it but instead she wanted me to meet these two brothers from Boston who would take us to a reggae concert in town. One of the boys offered me a joint and I eagerly inhaled it. I wanted to forget the scene I saw on The Lucky Irene. I wanted my version of Echo Beach to return.

That day was so hot and humid that it was difficult to breathe, and the smoke from the ganja smelled like burnt sugar. The singer was dressed in green and everyone in the audience held green stalks in their hands and swayed in rhythm to the music. We hitched a ride back to the hotel in an open truck filled with cats. The cats climbed all over my body and when it suddenly rained they nestled against our bodies for protection. The rain felt soft and warm against my face. In that moment, I didn't have to think about the man in the white suit. I didn't have to think about the boy from all those years ago getting slapped across the face. There was just the music, the rain, that moment, the simplicity of Jamaica being uncomplicated Jamaica. At sixteen, this was all I wanted.

III.

Susie's House was modeled after Rick's Café in Negril, supposedly the best place in all of Jamaica to watch a sunset. I was twenty-four, and on this holiday my parents had invited my fiancé, James, to join us.

I had met James at a bar after a group of us decided to have a drink after work. He was a lawyer who had gone to Harvard, he knew how to play tennis with my father, and could keep up with my parents' drinking. "Plenty of women would scratch out your eyes for that one," my mother told me once after her third martini. "You'd be a fool to lose him."

James had not wanted to visit Jamaica. He was not a tourist but an explorer. His usual trips were to exotic places like Sri Lanka or the Maldives, and sometimes he sold his photographs to magazines. But I wanted him to see Echo Beach. It was part of my history, and he needed to understand that.

James and I sat on the veranda overlooking the ocean. The couple next to us from Cleveland was betting on the exact moment the sun would sink away from sight. James said 6:01 and the woman promised us a bottle of champagne if we were right. James laughed and shook her hand. He was right. The sun now was a pink sliver vanishing into a blood-red sea. The show was greeted with appreciative murmurs. A waiter brought over a bottle of champagne. We shared the bottle with the other tourists there—honeymooners, an elderly couple celebrating their fortieth anniversary. The champagne was too warm and sweet but we didn't care. The bubbles went right to my head and I was floating.

James loved Jamaica in a way a tourist loves Jamaica: climbing Dun River Falls, bamboo rafting on the Martha Brae River, and visiting rum distilleries, where the samples were plentiful and James would always fall asleep as soon as we returned to the hotel. These expeditions exhausted me. I much preferred staying at the hotel, walking on the beach or visiting Trevor.

"I'm bored here," James said. "Why won't you go beyond the hotel gates?"

"I like being here at Echo Beach," I answered. Could he understand that this was not just a hotel but also a refuge for me when I was a child and an adolescent?

James pointed to the bathroom, which could have been cleaner and shook his head. "This is not Shangri-La, Claire," he told me, and then he threw me down on the bed and proceeded to take off all my clothes. Being here in Jamaica had made him more hot-blooded and the sex was dynamic. But after it was over, I felt hollow. Would this remain when we returned to Boston?

One morning James went parasailing with two other young men he had met at one of the rum distilleries. I declined to join him, and decided to visit Trevor at The Cypress Bar. He was busy serving beer to three college kids who all wore Toronto Maple Leaf sweatshirts. This was something I noticed Canadians did to make sure they weren't mistaken for Americans. The men were all laughing too loudly and were drunk even though it was only eleven in the morning. I could tell that their laughter bothered Trevor by the way he stood stiffly, and instead of joining the conversation only nodded his head. Trevor had aged well over the years. His hair was just beginning to glisten with thin silver threads. He still stood proudly at six foot two and the mirror behind him at the bar reflected his image so that he looked even two inches taller. I stood at the end of the bar, near the sliced limes and oranges, and waited for him. When he saw me, he didn't smile as I expected.

"Claire, why are you here?"

"What do you mean?" I asked. The day was not going as I planned. I had hoped that Trevor would invite me to the kitchen for a cup of tea and speak again of his childhood in England.

"I saw James earlier this morning. He said he was off to parasailing. I assumed you would join him."

I shook my head more vigorously than I realized. "No, I wanted to stay here. We have so much to catch up with, Trevor."

"Oh, Claire, you're not a little girl anymore. You need to be with the man you will marry." One of the Canadians shouted something. "Excuse me," he said, and he walked away without glancing back.

Tears stung my eyes. Why was I so foolish? I should be with James. I spent the rest of the afternoon in town buying useless souvenirs. When James returned, he was sunburnt and drunk. He and his friends had visited yet another local distillery. He went to sleep as I carefully made up my face for dinner. I thought about Trevor telling me I should be with my fiancé. He may have been right. James loved Jamaica, but I sensed that he was jealous of Trevor and our easy relationship. "He's just a bartender," James had said to me after the first time I introduced him to Trevor. "You talk to him like he's the owner of the hotel."

Our custom before dinner was that we would have a drink at The Cypress Bar. That afternoon, with James out cold, I wasn't so sure he would join me. But he woke up, took a long shower, and seemed to have sobered up. Luckily the group of Canadians was gone when we arrived at the bar. Trevor had a large smile on his face.

"How was the parasailing?" he asked James.

"How did you know?"

"Claire told me."

James stared at me in a way that made me feel cold. Trevor must have noticed because he added, "I told her that she should have joined you. More adventurous than staying here at the hotel."

"That's exactly right. See, Claire. Trevor knows what he's talking about. How about two Bacardis?"

I could still smell the scent of rum on James's breath.

"Do you really think we should?" I asked.

"This is our holiday," James said. "Enjoy. Right, Trevor?"

"Righto!" Trevor let out a low whistle and brought out two glasses and a bottle of Bacardi rum. "I propose a toast," Trevor announced. "A long and wonderful life to the two of you." Trevor poured until our glasses nearly overflowed and James drank the rum with one swift gulp. Two guests entered the bar. A woman wearing a silver turban asked Trevor to light her cigarette. A man in a straw hat was scolding his wife for paying too much money at the market. The smell of pina coladas was too sweet and sickening. James rattled the ice cubes in his glass and the sound reminded me of those blue beads spilling across that woman's porch so many years ago.

"Hey Trevor," James called out. Trevor was busy carefully carrying a tray of cocktails. "Trevor," he said louder, and then whistled.

"James, stop it," I told him in a lowered voice.

"Stop what? You're the one who needs to stop, Claire. You haven't relaxed once since we got here."

Trevor walked slowly to us, his eyes narrowed.

"Yes, what can I do for you?" he asked, slinging a tea towel across his shoulder.

James leaned in over the bar. His nose was sunburnt and his eyes were glazed the way they got when he drank too much. "How about joining us for dinner tonight?"

Trevor seemed to take a breath and slowly exhaled. "I appreciate your offer but that would be impossible."

"And why's that?" James demanded.

"You have your dinner in the hotel's dining room. The waiters are the only hotel staff allowed in the dining room."

"But Trevor, you'll be our guest. I will talk to the host. I'm sure he'll agree. If he doesn't, a twenty-dollar bill will surely help."

Trevor just shrugged, turned around and began to wipe the bar with the towel. I knew Trevor was right. The hotel staff was intensely competitive. Many envied his popularity with the guests. Yet it did seem silly that he was not allowed to join us for one night.

"We'll see you at seven," James said as he hopped off the stool. He quickly walked out of the bar, past the pool and headed toward the beach.

Trevor returned to me and gave me a glass of water. "Drink this, Claire. You don't want to be dehydrated in this heat."

I drank the cold water, started to speak and then stopped. I felt embarrassed and angry and desperately wanted to hide in the warmth of the kitchen and listen to Trevor's sentimental school songs. His eyes looked away from my face.

"You better find your fiancé," he told me.

I found James at the end of the beach, wading in the shallowest part of the sea. His shoes and socks were neatly folded a few feet away, though he had neglected to roll up his pants. His hair looked wet and fell in damp strands across his eyes. A glass bottom boat ride on a nearby dock made a sad creaking noise as it rolled upon the waves. I took off my sandals and tiptoed into the warm water.

"I love you, Claire," James said quietly as he touched my cheek.

I knew I should kiss him but instead I moved my face away. I was angry with myself and didn't completely understand why.

That night at the restaurant we sat at a table beneath a full moon and shimmering stars. The air was humid and the mosquitoes were particularly vicious. I wrapped a shawl about my shoulders but could still feel them burrowing beneath the cloth. Our waiter stood behind my chair, tapping his pen against his thigh. It was late and we had not yet ordered.

"He won't come," I told James yet again as he glanced at his watch.

"Oh yes he will."

James wore a white suit, reminding me of the Jamaican man so many years ago on the deck of The Lucky Irene. Irene had died but her yacht remained still moored on the dock, a vandalized ghost boat. The windows were shattered and the deck covered with broken glass. Why was it still here? It was said that during a full moon Irene's ghost could be seen dancing to the strains of unearthly music, her long shimmering scarf blowing in the wind. Our waiter sighed loudly as the dining room clock struck ten.

"There he is," James said in a loud voice.

Trevor stood at the end of the dining room. He was still wearing his bartender's uniform. He hesitated at the threshold.

"I'll talk to him," I told James.

"No, Claire. Stay where you are."

I watched James approach Trevor, and the men conversed with their heads bowed together. Then James clamped his hand on Trevor's shoulder and brought him over to the table. Trevor stood by his empty place, his hands clasped behind his back.

"Hello, Claire," Trevor began. "I was just telling James..."

"Sit down, Trevor," James told him.

"As I said before, I appreciate the offer but this will only cause trouble. The waiters don't like this."

"And why's that?" James asked impatiently.

"I belong in the bar. They belong in the dining room. Some would think I am here to steal their tips."

Trevor's forehead was wet with sweat, and his white shirt clung damply to his skin. The guests at the other tables were staring at us.

"I'm sorry. Thank you for the invite. Now you must excuse me." Trevor walked swiftly out of the dining room. I saw several waiters murmuring.

"Waiter," James called out. "We're ready to order."

"You're despicable," I said, standing up. "Torturing Trevor like that."

"Sit down, Claire and finish your drink," James snapped at me. "People are staring at you."

We ordered our dinner and finished the meal in silence. The next day I joined James at Dun River Falls but slipped on a rock and twisted my ankle. The bruise turned purple and swelled to the size of a golf ball. I spent two days alone in the hotel room as James took sailing lessons and played tennis. The lights in my room were always turned off and the shades drawn. Though I could already hear myself tell the story later when we got home, saying with a small laugh what a shame it was that I had sprained my ankle, the truth was that I wanted that time alone in the room. I reread my favorite Agatha Christie novels and spent time in the bath. In the distance, I could hear the calypso music that still played my favorite song: "Good Morning, Mr. Walker." I realized I loved Echo Beach more than James.

One night in bed, James tossed and turned, unable to sleep. I sensed his restlessness. Finally, he clicked on the bedside lamp and turned to me. His face looked grey and crumpled in the darkness.

"I'm going home tomorrow, Claire. I don't know why, but there's something I can't touch within you that is here on this island and here in this hotel. It's getting between us. I can feel it. Please tell me you'll join me."

I knew in that moment that I was supposed to talk with him, beg him to stay, at least pretend to cry—but I couldn't. James left that morning in the middle of a ferocious thunderstorm that made the island shake as if it were only a leaf in a tree. The walls of my bungalow shuddered as water trickled in a steady stream from a leak in my ceiling. Yet the next morning there was a rainbow so glorious that it brought tears to my eyes. I walked to the beach and buried my legs beneath the cool sand, vowing I could always return to Echo Beach. James was right. There was something here he couldn't touch.

IV.

The sun was relentless that holiday and dried the grass so that it snapped like twigs. I was now thirty, single, and living in a small apartment in Queens, New York. Jamaica still looked orange to me, even though I never took off my green-tinted glasses. My hotel window overlooked the sea and the bellboy had told me that sharks had been spotted in nearby waves. At night I thought I could see them, their fins flashing silver in the pearl moonlight.

The hotel was no longer called Echo Beach, but I refused to recognize its new name. Only the lobby had been remodeled as a pavilion with screens instead of windows. The screens were supposed to keep out the insects, but they still made their way through holes: mosquitoes, wasps and the occasional butterfly.

Trevor was surprised to see me. I was relieved he was still there. I had feared he would have moved on, a fear that went through me each time I returned to Echo Beach. Six years had passed since I had last seen him. I stood behind the door for a full minute before I had the courage to walk inside. The bar still smelled of sweet pineapples and coconut juice. A neon sign hung over the counter and the television set was tuned to CNN news. The bluish light from the television made the faces of the people at the bar look cruel. A skinny teenager wearing a t-shirt with the face of Bob Marley refilled the peanut dishes. Trevor was talking to a group of men wearing skimpy bathing suits and gold chains around their necks.

Trevor turned to refill a glass when he saw me. It seemed he had not aged at all except for a slight stoop to his shoulders. I watched his eyes squint slowly and then he grinned.

"Hello, Trevor," I said.

"Hello, dear Claire."

I was so relieved he had recognized me. He walked over and clasped my hand in his own.

"Dear me, I never thought I'd see you again, love."

"How are you, Trevor?"

"As well as can be. And your mother and father?"

"They both passed away."

Trevor lowered his eyes and was silent. Then he placed his hand on my shoulder. "I am so very sorry," he told me. "May God be with them."

Someone called out Trevor's name and he told me he would be right back. I sat on a hard stool and ate damp peanuts from a glass bowl. The boy in the Bob Marley t-shirt stared at me. Strong gusts suddenly blew in from the sea and knocked over several empty glasses.

"Jimmy," Trevor shouted to the boy. "Close that window!" Trevor returned to me, his head turned to the side as if looking for someone. "Where is James?"

"I haven't seen him in years," I told him.

At that moment, a red butterfly fluttered in. It blew in suddenly and landed on top of a beer glass.

"It's lost," said Trevor, cupping the butterfly in his hand. "We don't have this kind of butterfly here in Jamaica. It must be from somewhere across the sea, far away."

The boy was having difficulty with the shutters. Trevor shook his head and went over to help him. "Jimmy," he told him. "Why don't you go and serve that lovely lady a drink."

"Yes sir. The boy's accent sounded like a poor imitation of Trevor's own. He even snapped his fingers the way Trevor used to long ago.

"What will you have Miss?"

"A Manhattan."

The boy began mixing my drink, whistling shrilly through his teeth. Trevor came over at several points, showing him the correct way to make the cocktail.

"How much do I owe you?" I asked Trevor.

"This is on the house. Always has been, my dear."

I finished the drink quickly and asked for another. Trevor looked at the empty glass and lifted his gaze to my face.

"It looks as if you had a few before you even came in, Claire."

"Please, Trevor. I'm not fifteen anymore."

"Why don't I bring you a nice cup of tea? You always liked the way I made tea."

I laughed. He was right. I did have a few drinks on the airplane, and seeing the new sign on the hotel had been upsetting, and made me want more alcohol.

"Tea? In this weather? Oh Trevor, you'll never leave England, will you?"

"Then I'll just make tea for myself," he said lightly as he quickly turned and walked toward the kitchen.

I wanted to apologize but it was too late. Of course I wanted the tea, and also the chance to be alone with Trevor. I wished I could take my words back.

The bar was getting crowded. I shivered even though it wasn't cool and placed my sweater over my shoulders. Behind me, something bumped and I quickly turned around.

"Would the missis care for another drink?"

Jimmy stood so close to me that I could smell the tobacco under his breath.

"Another Manhattan," I said, hearing myself stumble over the words.

"Very good," he murmured.

I felt the need for a cigarette and reached behind my chair for my bag. My Marlboro pack was gone. So seemed to be my wallet. I swore under my breath. There wasn't much money in the wallet and my passport was stored safely in another bag. But the photographs of my parents were important to me and there were credit cards and a driver's license in it that would be difficult to replace. I was certain I'd had it when I walked into the bar. I turned my bag upside down and began sorting through the contents: tissues, lipsticks, coins, and a luggage receipt.

"Is anything wrong Miss?" I heard a voice say. I looked up and saw a tall security guard staring at me.

"I'm sorry. I can't seem to find my wallet."

"Were you just talking to that boy over there?" The guard pointed over to Jimmy who was standing by the entrance, helping to sort through luggage.

"Yes," I began. "But he—"

"You!" the security guard shouted. Jimmy walked over, his hands in his pockets.

"Who are you?" the guard asked him.

"My name is Jimmy Hughes," the boy said. "I started just last week. I help Trevor in The Cypress Bar." Jimmy looked nervous. Sweat dotted his forehead. "He's teaching me how to bartend."

"I need to search you."

"Please," I told the security guard. "I'm sure I'll find it."

"We need to search this man."

"I'll—I'll talk to Trevor," I said falteringly.

"Wait for him. He'll sort it out."

But the guard had already taken the boy by the arm and disappeared down a hall.

I returned to the lobby and stood next to a large potted palm. My heart was racing. What had just happened? If I hadn't had so many drinks, I could have handled the situation better. A small calypso band had been set up and several couples were dancing around the steel drums. The tune was bright and fast and it wasn't until the refrain that I recognized it. *"Good morning, Mrs. Walker..."* But it didn't sound the same as I remembered. The words seemed different and the beat too fast. Yet the song moved something so deep inside me that I had to lean against the wall to catch my breath. For a brief moment I forgot about the wallet. Nothing mattered except that I was here at Echo Beach.

After a few minutes, I saw Trevor walking toward me. His eyes were lowered to the ground, and only when he stood in front of me did he lift his gaze.

"Listen, Trevor," I said, slightly swaying the music. "Listen to what they're playing."

"What are you talking about Claire?" he said angrily. I had never heard him raise his voice before and I flinched. His shoulders were shaking. "Do you realize what you have done? You've made a terrible accusation that has ruined the boy."

I stood there in shock. "But I didn't say anything. The guard..."

"You're a white woman saying that her wallet is missing. You should have found me and told me. I know that boy's parents. They are good people."

"I will find that guard," I told Trevor, standing up. "I'll tell him Jimmy is innocent."

"Whether it's true or not, they have fired him. He will not find work at any of the hotels here."

"Oh Trevor, I'm sorry," I said, trying to keep my words steady. "Maybe I did leave the wallet somewhere. I just want to be here. At Echo Beach. With you. That's all that matters."

"With me?" he asked, jabbing a finger at his chest. "You know nothing about me!" I had never heard him raise his voice before. The whites of his eyes were gleaming. "Have you ever asked about my family? My wife? Have you ever met a Jamaican who wasn't here to serve you? To serve all of you? What do you know about this country? The people here? How long are you even here in Jamaica? One week every few years? My God, Claire, you are trying to find something that is not real. The hotel is not even called Echo Beach anymore."

"I know." I turned around because I didn't want him to see my tears.

"Go home," he said calmly. "There is nothing for you here. Go home, Claire."

Watching Trevor leave, I noticed that his back was very stiff and straight. The noise from the steel band made my head ache and I walked out of the lobby toward the beach. The sun stunned my eyes. I wiped my wet face with my sleeve. I reached into my purse for my sunglasses and froze. My hands had touched my wallet. It was hiding beneath my boarding pass. I felt its smooth leather.

I looked out at the ocean and felt the blood in my face. I would find the hotel manager and demand that Jimmy not lose his job. But would they listen to me? I was just a tourist—a silly ignorant visitor to a place that could never be my sanctuary. I remember that little boy I had followed on the beach who had been slapped. That was my fault. Trevor had told me that the boy's family could be in trouble with the police. I had done it again with Jimmy. There was no place for me here. Echo Beach had always been an illusion. I would leave tomorrow.

In the haze I thought I saw that ghost vessel, The Lucky Irene, still tethered to the dock, restored to its previous glory. Torches of light shone on the deck, and I could hear peals of laughter and the clinking of glasses. And then I saw him. The man in the white suit. Irene's "friend." He had not aged at all. His suit fit him perfectly and he still wore a slender gold watch. That watch glittered in the light as he slowly waved to me. His mouth moved but the ocean was too noisy, and I couldn't hear if he said hello or goodbye.

CPSIA information can be obtained
at www.ICGtesting.com
Printed in the USA
LVHW101131040323
740851LV00002B/95